William Shakespeare's The Winter's Tale: A Retelling in Prose

David Bruce

Published by David Bruce, 2022.

WILLIAM SHAKESPEARE'S THE WINTER'S TALE: A RETELLING IN PROSE

First edition. July 29, 2022.

Copyright © 2022 David Bruce.

ISBN: 979-8201782559

Written by David Bruce.

Table of Contents

Dedication

Dedicated to Carl Eugene Bruce and Josephine Saturday Bruce

My father, Carl Eugene Bruce, died on 24 October 2013. He used to work for Ohio Power, and at one time, his job was to shut off the electricity of people who had not paid their bills. He sometimes would find a home with an impoverished mother and some children. Instead of shutting off their electricity, he would tell the mother that she needed to pay her bill or soon her electricity would be shut off. He would write on a form that no one was home when he stopped by because if no one was home he did not have to shut off their electricity.

The best good deed that anyone ever did for my father occurred after a storm that knocked down many power lines. He and other linemen worked long hours and got wet and cold. Their feet were freezing because water got into their boots and soaked their socks. Fortunately, a kind woman gave my father and the other linemen dry socks to wear.

My mother, Josephine Saturday Bruce, died on 14 June 2003. She used to work at a store that sold clothing. One day, an impoverished mother with a baby clothed in rags walked into the store and started shoplifting in an interesting way: The mother took the rags off her baby and dressed the infant in new clothing. My mother knew that this mother could not afford to buy the clothing, but she helped the mother dress her baby and then she watched as the mother walked out of the store without paying.

***

The doing of good deeds is important. As a free person, you can choose to live your life as a good person or as a bad person. To be a good person, do good deeds. To be a bad person, do bad deeds. If you do good deeds, you will become good. If you do bad deeds, you will become bad. To become the person you want to be, act as if you already are that kind of person. Each of us chooses what kind of person we will become. To become a good person, do the things a good person does. To become a bad person, do the things a bad person does. The opportunity to take action to become the kind of person you want to be is yours.

Human beings have free will. According to the Babylonian Niddah 16b, whenever a baby is to be conceived, the Lailah (angel in charge of contraception) takes the drop of semen that will result in the conception and asks God, "Sovereign of the Universe, what is going to be the fate of this drop? Will it develop into a robust or into a weak person? An intelligent or a stupid person? A wealthy or a poor person?" The Lailah asks all these questions, but it does not ask, "Will it develop into a righteous or a wicked person?" The answer to that question lies in the decisions to be freely made by the human being that is the result of the conception.

A Buddhist monk visiting a class wrote this on the chalkboard: "EVERYONE WANTS TO SAVE THE WORLD, BUT NO ONE WANTS TO HELP MOM DO THE DISHES." The students laughed, but the monk then said, "Statistically, it's highly unlikely that any of you will ever have the opportunity to run into a burning orphanage and rescue an infant. But, in the smallest gesture of kindness — a warm smile, holding the door for the person behind you, shoveling the driveway of the elderly person next door — you have committed an act of immeasurable profundity, because to each of us, our life is our universe."

In her book titled *I Have Chosen to Stay and Fight*, comedian Margaret Cho writes, "I believe that we get complimentary snack-size portions of the afterlife, and we all receive them in a different way." For Ms. Cho, many of her snack-size portions of the afterlife come in hip hop music. Other people get different snack-size portions of the afterlife, and we all must be on the lookout for them when they come our way. And perhaps doing good deeds and experiencing good deeds are snack-size portions of the afterlife.

The Zen master Gisan was taking a bath. The water was too hot, so he asked a student to add some cold water to the bath. The student brought a bucket of cold water, added some cold water to the bath, and then threw the rest of the water on a rocky path. Gisan scolded the student: "Everything can be used. Why did you waste the rest of the water by pouring it on the path? There are some plants nearby which could have used the water. What right do you have to waste even a drop of water?" The student became enlightened and changed his name to Tekisui, which means "Drop of Water."

Educate Yourself
Read Like A Wolf Eats
Be Excellent to Each Other
Books Then, Books Now, Books Forever

***

In this retelling, as in all my retellings, I have tried to make the work of literature accessible to modern readers who may lack the knowledge about mythology, religion, and history that the literary work's contemporary audience had.

Do you know a language other than English? If you do, I give you permission to translate this book, copyright your translation, publish or self-publish it, and keep all the royalties for yourself. (Do give me credit, of course, for the original retelling.)

I would like to see my retellings of classic literature used in schools, so I give permission to the country of Finland (and all other countries) to give copies of this book to all students forever. I also give permission to the state of Texas (and all other states) to give copies of this book to all students forever. I also give permission to all teachers to give copies of this book to all students forever.

Teachers need not actually teach my retellings. Teachers are welcome to give students copies of my eBooks as background material. For example, if they are teaching Homer's *Iliad* and *Odyssey*, teachers are welcome to give students copies of my *Virgil's* Aeneid: *A Retelling in Prose* and tell students, "Here's another ancient epic you may want to read in your spare time."

CAST OF CHARACTERS

MALE CHARACTERS

LEONTES, King of Sicily.

MAMILLIUS, young Prince of Sicily.

CAMILLO, ANTIGONUS, CLEOMENES, and DION, Lords of Sicily.

POLIXENES, King of Bohemia.

FLORIZEL, his Son.

ARCHIDAMUS, a Lord of Bohemia.

A Mariner.

A Jailer.

An old Shepherd, reputed Father of Perdita.

CLOWN, his Son. The son of the shepherd is a Clown character — a comic character. In this retelling of the play, I made "Clown" his nickname because I did not want to continually refer to him as the old shepherd's son. Shakespeare did not use "Clown" as a nickname.

Servant to the old Shepherd.

AUTOLYCUS, a Rogue.

FEMALE CHARACTERS

HERMIONE, Queen to Leontes, King of Sicily.

PERDITA, Daughter to Leontes and Hermione.

PAULINA, Wife to Antigonus.

EMILIA, a Lady.

Other Ladies, attending the Queen.

MOPSA and DORCAS, Shepherdesses.

MINOR CHARACTERS

Sicilian Lords and Ladies, Attendants, Guards, Herdsmen dressed as Satyrs, Shepherds, Shepherdesses, etc.

Time, as Chorus.

SCENE

Sometimes in Sicily, sometimes in Bohemia.

CHAPTER 1
— 1.1 —

In an antechamber in the palace of Leontes, King of Sicily, two courtiers were conversing. Archidamus was a courtier from Bohemia, and Camillo was a courtier from Sicily. For the past nine months, Polixenes, King of Bohemia, had been visiting Leontes, a childhood friend. Now, however, Polixenes wanted to return to his Kingdom. The two courtiers were formal as they spoke to each other.

Archidamus said, "If you should happen, Camillo, to visit Bohemia on a similar diplomatic visit such as that on which my services are now engaged, you shall see, as I have said, great differences between our Bohemia and your Sicily."

Archidamus was speaking truer than he knew. Soon, a great difference — a great quarrel — would arise between the King of Bohemia and the King of Sicily.

"I think that this coming summer the King of Sicily intends to pay Bohemia the visit that he justly and reciprocally owes him," Camillo replied.

"During that visit, our hospitality shall shame us because of its poverty; however, our good will toward you shall excuse us because indeed —"

"Please —" Camillo interrupted.

Archidamus interrupted Camillo: "Truly, I speak what I know. We cannot entertain you the way that you have entertained us with such magnificence — which is so rare that I don't know what to say. We will give you sleep-inducing drinks so that you, unaware of the insufficiency of our hospitality, may, although you cannot praise us, criticize us as little as possible."

"You pay a great deal too much for what's given freely," Camillo said. "I want to freely pay you a compliment, but you will not allow me to."

"Believe me, I speak what I know to be true, and my honesty makes me say it to you," Archidamus said.

Camillo, the courtier from Sicily, replied, "The King of Sicily cannot be too kind to the King of Bohemia. They were trained together in their childhoods; and there rooted between them then such an affection that cannot choose but branch now."

Camillo was also speaking truer than he knew. "Trained" was a horticultural word, as were "rooted" and "branch," the latter of which had two meanings: 1) to branch out, aka produce branches and grow, and 2) to go in two different directions. Soon, the two Kings would quarrel and go in two different directions.

He continued, "They grew up, and then their high position and duties and obligations in adult life caused them to be separated; however, the two kept in touch. Their deputies have done an excellent job of delivering gifts and letters and making friendly embassies from one King to the other King. The two Kings, although in different countries, have seemed to be together. Although separated from each other, they have seemed to shake hands over a vast ocean, and embraced, as it were, from the ends of the Earth. May the Heavens help their friendship to continue!"

"I think there is nothing in the world — such as malice and evil will or any factual matter — that can stop their friendship," Archidamus said.

The two courtiers had been speaking formally, but now they loosened up and soon they began to joke with each other.

Archidamus said, "You have an inexpressibly great comfort in your young Prince Mamillius: He is a gentleman of the greatest promise who ever came into my notice."

"I very much agree with you," Camillo said. "We have great hopes for him. He is a gallant child: one who indeed is a tonic for all the citizens of Sicily. He makes old hearts fresh. Old people who walked with crutches before he was born hope to stay alive long enough to see him become a man."

"If not for that desire, would they be content to die?"

"Yes, if there were no other excuse why they should desire to live."

"If King Leontes had no son, they would desire to live on crutches until he had a son," Archidamus said.

In a room of state in the palace were Leontes, King of Sicily; Hermione, his wife; Mamillius, their son; Polixenes, King of Bohemia; Camillo, a courtier from Sicily; and some attendants.

Using the royal plural, King Polixenes said, "Shepherds have seen the Moon, the watery star that controls the tides, go through nine cycles since we left our throne without an occupant. I have been away from Bohemia for nine months. We could thank you, Leontes, my brother King, nine months for your hospitality, but yet we should, for perpetuity, still owe you thanks. Therefore, let my 'We thank you' be like a zero that when added to other numbers multiply by many thousands the numbers that go before it. Let my one 'We thank you' stand for all the many thousand thank-yous we owe to you."

King Leontes replied, "Do not say thanks now; say thanks when you depart from Sicily."

"Sir, that will be tomorrow," King Polixenes said. "My fears make me ask what may happen or what trouble may breed because of my long absence from Bohemia. I fear that sneaping, aka cutting, winds may blow at home — winds that will make us say, 'Yes, we had just cause to be afraid of what might happen during our long absence.' Besides, I have stayed too long here and I am tiring your majesty."

"We are tougher, brother King," Leontes said, "than any 'trouble' you can give us."

"I can no longer stay here. I must return home."

"Stay one week longer," King Leontes requested.

"Truly I must leave tomorrow."

"We will compromise and split the time between us," King Leontes said. "Stay half a week longer and know that I won't take 'no' for an answer."

"Do not press me to stay," King Polixenes said. "Please do not press me. No tongue that moves, none — none in the world — could persuade me as quickly as yours. You could persuade me now if you had a good reason for needing me here, even if I had a good reason to deny your request. My affairs drag me homeward: I am needed there. If you were to hinder me and prevent me from leaving, it would be like a whip to me even if you wanted me to stay longer because of our friendship. My stay here costs you expense and trouble. To save you from both, I will leave. Farewell, our brother."

King Leontes said to his wife, Hermione, "Tongue-tied, our Queen? Speak to him."

"I had thought, sir, to have held my peace until you had drawn from him oaths not to stay and then I would come and save the day," Hermione said. "You, sir, try to persuade him too coldly. Tell him that you are sure that everything in Bohemia is well. This is supported by the news that we received yesterday from Bohemia. Tell him this. By doing so, you will beat his best argument for returning to his home."

"Well said, Hermione," King Leontes said.

"Another good and strong argument for him to return to his home," Hermione said, "is for him to say that he longs to see his son. If that is his reason for going, let him say so then, and let him go. If he swears that that is his reason for leaving, he shall not stay here. We women will thwack him away from here. We will hit him with the distaffs that we use when we spin wool."

Hermione said to King Polixenes, "Yet of your royal presence I'll venture to borrow a week. When in Bohemia you entertain my lord, I'll pay back the loan of a week by giving him permission in advance to stay in Bohemia a month longer than the time fixed for his departure back to Sicily."

She added, "But indeed, Leontes, my husband, I love you not a jot less than any woman who loves her lord and husband."

King Leontes walked over to his son.

Hermione asked King Polixenes, "You'll stay?"

"No, madam."

"Won't you stay?"

"I cannot, truly and verily."

"Verily!" Hermione exclaimed. "You put me off with limp and weak vows; but I, even if you were to try to shake stars out of the sky with your oaths, would still say, 'Sir, you shall not go.' Verily, you shall not go. A lady's 'verily' is as potent as a lord's. Women can make oaths as strong as the oaths of men. Do you still insist on going? You will force me to keep you as a prisoner, not as a guest. In that case you shall pay your fees when you depart the way that a prisoner pays a fee to the jailer when he departs, and you will save your thanks.

What do you say now? Will you be my prisoner or my guest? I swear by your dread 'verily' that you will be one of them."

"In that case, I will be your guest, madam," King Polixenes replied. "To be your prisoner implies that I would have offended you by committing an offense. I would find it less easy to commit an offense than you would to punish it."

"So I will not be your jailer then, but instead your kind hostess," Hermione said. "Come, I'll ask you questions about my husband's tricks and yours when you were boys."

She asked him, "You were pretty lordings — fine young boys — then?"

"We were, fair Queen," King Polixenes said. "We were two lads who thought there was nothing more to come except a day tomorrow that was like the day today. We thought that we would be boys forever."

"Was not my lord — my husband — the greater rascal of you two?"

"We were like twin lambs frisking in the Sun, and each of us bleated at the other. What we exchanged was innocence for innocence; we knew nothing about evil and we did not dream that anyone committed evil acts. Had we pursued that life, and had our youthful innocence never been replaced by mature thoughts because of our growing up, we should have answered Heaven boldly 'not guilty of personal sin' on the Day of Judgment. Our only sin would have been the original sin we inherited from Adam, the first man."

"By this I gather that you have tripped and sinned since you were boys," Hermione said.

"My most sacred lady!" King Polixenes said. "Temptations have since then come to us. In those unfledged days my wife was only a girl, and your precious self had then not crossed the eyes of my young playfellow."

"May Heaven help us!" Hermione said. "Don't continue speaking, lest you say that your Queen and I are devils who made you two sin. Yet go on. The offences that your Queen and I have made you do we'll answer to, assuming that you first sinned with us and that you continued to sin with us and that you did not sin with anyone but us."

Leontes came closer to them and asked Hermione, "Is he won over yet?"

"He'll stay, my lord."

"At my request, he would not," King Leontes said. "Hermione, my dearest, you have never spoken better and for a better purpose."

"Never?" she replied.

"Never, except once," her husband said.

"What! Have I twice spoken well? When was the other time? Please tell me. Cram us women with praise, and make us as fat as tame things such as household pets. One good deed that is not praised slaughters a thousand good deeds that would have been done if that good deed had been praised. Praises are the wages of women. You may ride us with one soft kiss a thousand furlongs before we would gallop an acre as a result of being spurred. You will receive more from a woman if you treat her with kindness than if you treat her harshly.

"But to get to the point: My most recent good deed with words was to persuade King Polixenes to stay here longer. What was my first good deed with words? It has an elder sister — it was done previously to this good deed unless I mistake you. I hope that my other good deed has won me grace and favor. Once before today I spoke to the purpose. When? Tell me. I long to know."

"Why, that was when three crabbed months had soured themselves to death," King Leontes said. "It took me three months before I could make you open your white hand and accept my hand. When I succeeded, then you uttered, 'I am yours forever.' At that time, you agreed to marry me."

"That good deed brought me grace indeed," Hermione said. "Why — look at that! — I have spoken to the purpose twice. Once I forever earned a royal husband; the other time I earned for a longer time the presence of a friend."

In this society, the word "friend" could be used to mean "lover" instead of its usual meaning.

A man can fall in love with a glance; a man can also become jealous with a glance. Such feelings can be incredibly strong.

Hermione took King Polixenes' hand.

Seeing this, King Leontes instantly became jealous and thought, *They are too hot, too hot! To mingle friendship too far is mingling bloods. A man and a woman who take friendship too far end up in bed together and mingle their bodily fluids. I have* tremor cordis — *a trembling of my heart — in me. My heart dances, but not for joy — not for joy. This hospitality can have an innocent face. This liberty can come from sincerity, from generosity, and from a warm heart. It can well become the agent — Hermione, who may simply be a good hostess. I grant all that, but Hermione and King Polixenes are now paddling palms and pinching fingers — they are holding hands. And they are smiling at each other as if they were smiling into a mirror, and they are sighing deep sighs like those of a dying deer. This is hospitality that my heart does not like — or my brows! I can almost feel the horns of a cuckold growing from my brows!*

King Leontes went over to his son and asked him, "Mamillius, are you my boy?"

"Yes, my good lord."

"So you are, in faith," King Leontes said. "Why, that's my bawcock, aka fine fellow. What, have you smudged your nose? They say that your nose is a copy of mine. Come, young captain, we must be neat."

In this society, cuckolds — men with unfaithful wives — were said to have invisible horns growing on their forehead.

King Leontes thought a moment about the horns of a cuckold, and he remembered that one meaning of the word "neat" in their society was "cattle." Many cattle have horns.

He added, "Not neat, but we must be clean, captain. The steer, the heifer, and the calf are all called 'neat.'"

King Leontes looked over at his wife, Hermione, and King Polixenes, who were still holding hands.

He said, "She is still virginalling upon his palm!"

The virginals was a keyboard instrument that women played.

He said to his son, "How are you, you playful calf! Are you my calf?"

"Yes, if you want me to be, my lord," Mamillius said.

"You lack a rough head and the shoots that I have, so you are not exactly like me," King Leontes said.

By "shoots," he may have meant his beard — or the horns that he imagined to be growing from his head.

He continued, "Yet they say we are almost as alike as eggs. Women say so; women will say anything. They are as false as dyed black clothing that hides the real color. They are as false as wind and water — the words of a woman are written on wind and running water. They are as false as the dice of a gambler who recognizes no distinction between what is mine and what he wants to be his. Yet it is true to say that this boy looks like me.

"Come, sir page, look at me with your sky-blue eyes, sweet villain! You are very dear to me! You are a piece of me!"

He began to wonder if Hermione were unfaithful to him: *Can your dam — is it possible?*

A dam is an animal's mother. King Leontes was unwilling to think of his wife as human.

He thought, *Jealousy! Your intensity stabs the center of my being and heart! You make it possible to think things that were not thought to be possible. You communicate with dreams and illusions — but how can this be? You join and act in concert with what is unreal, and so you are able to join and act in concert with nothing. You make me think things that I thought not to be possible. Since you can do this, it becomes very believable that you may join and act in concert with something that is real. You have made me think that things that I thought to be impossible are in fact quite possible, and those things go beyond what is permitted — my wife is having an affair with my best friend! I find this to be true, and that has infected my brains and caused horns to grow on my brows.*

King Leontes realized that jealousy is often not justified, but he believed that in his case it was justified.

King Polixenes looked at King Leontes and asked Hermione, "What is wrong with your husband?"

"He seems somewhat unsettled," Hermione replied.

"How are you, my lord?" King Polixenes asked. "How do you feel? How is it with you, my best friend and brother and fellow King?"

Hermione said to her husband, "You look as if you have a lot on your mind. Are you angry about something, my lord?"

King Leontes replied, "No, truly I am not angry. Sometimes nature will betray its folly, its tenderness, and show that it is silly and sentimental. In doing so, it makes itself a laughingstock to people who lack sentimentality.

"Looking at the lineaments of my boy's face, I thought I had gone back twenty-three years, and I saw myself as a boy not yet old enough to wear pants. I was wearing my green velvet coat of the type that both young boys and young girls wear. My dagger was sheathed, lest it should bite its master, and so prove, as ornaments often do, to be dangerous. My dagger then was for show, not for use.

"How like, I thought, I then was to this kernel, this unripe peapod, this young gentleman, my son."

He asked his son, "My honest friend, will you take eggs for money?"

This was a proverbial expression that literally meant, Will you accept inexpensive goods rather than money? Figuratively, it meant, Will you allow yourself to be imposed upon?

Mamillius replied, "No, my lord, I'll fight."

This answer relieved King Leontes because this answer was the one that he would give. His son was like him both physically and mentally. His son was honest in two senses: He was honorable and legitimate.

"You will!" King Leontes happily exclaimed. "Why, good luck to you! May your lot in life be that of a happy man!"

He asked King Polixenes, "My brother King, are you as fond of your young Prince as we are of ours?"

"When I am at home, sir, my son keeps me busy and he is everything to me. He makes me laugh, and I am seriously concerned about his wellbeing. At one time he is my sworn friend, and at another time he is my enemy. He is my parasite who eats at my table, he is my soldier, he is my statesman — he is everything to me. By making me happy, he makes a day in July as short as a day in December. And with his varying childish whims he cures in me thoughts that would thicken my blood and make me sluggish and depressed."

"My own young squire, aka son, does the same things for me," King Leontes said. "My son and I will walk, my lord, and leave you and my wife to your graver and more mature steps.

"Hermione, show how you love us in our brother King's welcome. Let what is dear in Sicily be cheap. Next to yourself and my young rover here, King Polixenes is heir apparent — the person closest to my heart."

"If you want us, we will be in the garden," Hermione replied. "Shall we wait for you there?"

"Do whatever you please," King Leontes replied. "You'll be found as long as you are beneath the sky."

He thought, *By "found," I mean "found out." I am angling now, although you do not see me giving you line. I am giving you enough rope to hang yourself. Go on! Go on! Look at how my wife holds up her beak, her bill, her mouth, to him! And she takes his arm in hers with the boldness of a wife taking her approving husband's arm!*

King Polixenes, Hermione, and the attendants exited.

King Leontes thought, *My wife is gone already! She is lost to me, and she has fallen into sin by committing adultery with King Polixenes. The evidence for her adultery is as solid as an inch-thick board. She is knee-deep in sin. Most people are over head and ears in love, but I am over head and ears a forked one — the horns of a cuckold fork out of my forehead!*

He said to his son, "Go, play, boy, play."

He thought, *Your mother plays and commits adultery, and I play a part, too. I pretend to be an uncuckolded husband. I play so disgraced a part that I will be hissed to my grave like a bad actor being hissed off the stage. Contempt and clamor will be my funeral bell.*

He said again, "Go, play, boy, play."

He thought, *There have been, or I am much deceived, cuckolds before now; and many a man exists, even at this present time, right now while I think this, who holds his wife by the arm and little thinks that he has been sluiced in his absence and his pond fished by his nearest neighbor, by Sir Smile, his neighbor.*

"Sluiced" means "showered with water," but the "water" that King Leontes was thinking about was semen. He was also using the word "pond" as a synonym for "vagina." He would do the same thing with the word "gate."

He thought, *There's comfort in thinking that I am not the only cuckold. Other men have gates and those gates are opened, as mine is, against their will. If all men who have adulteress wives were to despair, a tenth of mankind would hang themselves. No medicine can cure a cuckold. Adultery is like a bawdy planet that in astrological terms will strike whenever it is in the ascendant. This planet is powerful — believe it! — in the east, west, north, and south. Let us realize that no vagina can be barricaded; a vagina will let in and out the enemy with bag and baggage — with scrotum and its contents. Many thousands of us have the disease of cuckoldry and don't know it.*

He said to his son, "How are you, boy?"

"I am like you, they say."

"Why, that's some comfort," King Leontes said.

He noticed a man and said, "What, is that my courtier Camillo there?"

"Yes, my good lord," Camillo replied.

King Leontes said, "Go play, Mamillius; you are an honest man."

Mamillius departed, and King Leontes thought, *You are legitimate; you are my son.*

King Leontes said, "Camillo, this great sir — King Polixenes — will stay a while longer."

"You had much trouble to make his anchor hold," Camillo replied. "When you cast the anchor out, it always dragged the bottom and came back."

"Did you see that?" King Leontes asked.

"King Polixenes would not stay here longer when you asked him to," Camillo said. "He always insisted that his reasons for returning to his Kingdom were more important."

"Did you perceive that?" King Leontes asked.

He thought, *They are already aware that I am a cuckold. They are whispering in corners, "The King of Sicily is a so-and-so."*

He did not want to put the word "cuckold" in the mouth of his subjects.

He thought, *News of my cuckoldry must have been known for a long time if I am the last to learn it.*

He asked, "How did it come to be, Camillo, that King Polixenes finally agreed to stay longer here?"

Camillo replied, "He agreed to stay longer because Queen Hermione asked him to stay longer."

"At the Queen's — so be it. 'Good' should be pertinent here, but as it happens, it is not. Did any other intelligent head but yours notice that? I ask because your intelligence is absorbent and draws in more information than the 'intelligence' of any common blockheads. No one noticed, I suppose, except some individuals of exceptional intelligence? People of lower intelligence are perhaps totally unaware of this business? Tell me what you think."

Camillo was puzzled by the questions. He was completely unaware of any suggestion that Queen Hermione had ever even thought of committing adultery.

He said, "Business, my lord? I think that most people understand that King Polixenes of Bohemia will stay here longer."

"What!" Leontes said.

Camillo repeated, "King Polixenes of Bohemia will stay here longer."

"Yes, but why?" King Leontes asked.

"To satisfy your Highness and the entreaties of our most gracious Queen Hermione."

"Satisfy! The entreaties of your Queen! Satisfy!" King Leontes exclaimed.

He was thinking of sexual satisfaction.

He said, "That's enough! I have trusted you, Camillo, with all the personal things nearest to my heart, as well as my thoughts about the affairs of state. I have confessed my feelings to you, and like a priest you have cleansed my bosom. I have departed from you like a reformed penitent."

He began to use the royal plural: "But we have been deceived in your integrity, deceived in that which only seems to be integrity."

"God forbid, my lord!" Camillo said.

"To say more on this subject," King Leontes said, "you are not honest, or, if you incline toward honesty, you are a coward. Your cowardice hamstrings your honesty, preventing it from doing what needs to be done. If that is not true, then you must be a servant whom I trust in serious matters but who is negligent. Or you may be a fool who sees a game played for high stakes — you actually see someone win the prize and yet you do not believe the game was played for real."

King Leontes was thinking that perhaps Camillo believed that what was really a seduction was instead a harmless flirtation.

"My gracious lord," Camillo said, "I may be negligent, foolish, and fearful. No man is completely free of each of these. In the infinite doings of the world, sometimes a man will be negligent, foolish, and fearful.

"However, in your affairs, my lord, if ever I was willfully negligent, it was due to my foolishness, and if ever I willfully played the fool, it was due to my negligence — I did not understand how important the matter was. If ever I was fearful to do a thing that I doubted would achieve the desired end, a thing that, once done, did in fact achieve the desired result and was clearly what needed to be done, mine was a fear that often infects the wisest.

"My lord, honesty is never free of such allowed infirmities as these. All of us make mistakes.

"But I beg your grace to be plainer with me; let me know specifically what you think that I have done wrong. If I deny doing it, then take my word that I am not guilty of it."

King Leontes replied, "Haven't you seen, Camillo, but there is no doubt that you have, for if you haven't, then the lens of your eye is thicker than a cuckold's horn ... or heard, for rumor cannot keep quiet about something that can be so easily seen ... or thought, for any man who is capable of thought must have thought this — that my wife is slippery?

"If you will admit that you have — for to admit that you have not is to say that you are incapable of seeing, hearing, and thinking — then say that my wife is a hobby-horse, a whore, that anyone can ride. Say that she deserves a name as rank as any lower-class wench who puts out even before she is engaged. Say it and swear that it is true."

Shocked, Camillo said, "I will not be a bystander who hears my Queen so clouded and criticized with words — not without immediately speaking up in her defense and defending her.

"Curse my heart, but you have never spoken what becomes you less than this which you have spoken just now."

Camillo was angry. He had not used "my lord" or "your grace" or "sir" when speaking to the King. He had also forcefully criticized his King — as a good advisor should have done. Still, he knew that he should have called King Leontes "my lord" or "your grace," and he believed that he could have expressed his criticism in other, less offensive words.

He said, "To reiterate what I have just said would be a sin as deep as the sin of the words you just spoke, although the criticism I made of you is true."

King Leontes produced his "evidence" that his wife and King Polixenes were having an affair: "Is whispering nothing? Is leaning cheek to cheek? Is touching noses during a kiss? Is kissing with the inside of the lips? Is stopping the act of laughing with a sigh? Here is infallible evidence of breaking honesty. Is playing footsie nothing? Hiding in corners? Wishing that clocks were swifter? Wishing that hours were minutes? Wishing that noon was midnight? Wishing that all eyes were blind with cataracts except theirs, theirs only, so they could be wicked without being seen? Is this nothing?

"Why, if so, then the world and all that's in it is nothing. The covering sky is nothing. The King of Bohemia is nothing. My wife is nothing. These nothings are nothing, if this is nothing."

"My good lord, be cured of this diseased opinion of yours, and quickly, because this diseased opinion is very dangerous," Camillo said. "Don't be jealous."

"Even if it is dangerous to say so, it is true, Camillo," King Leontes said. "It is true. My wife is having an affair."

"No, no, my lord," Camillo replied.

"It is true," King Leontes said. "You lie! You lie! I say that you lie, Camillo, and I hate you. I say that you are a gross lout and a mindless slave. Or else you are a vacillating opportunist. You see at the same time good and evil, and you incline toward one or the other in accordance with which one will most benefit you.

"If my wife's heart — the seat of her passion — was as infected as her life, she would not live even an hour longer."

"Who infects her with passion?" Camillo asked.

"Why, he who wears her like a miniature portrait, hanging around his neck," King Leontes said. "The King of Bohemia, who, if I had loyal servants around me, who had the eyes to see that what affects my honor also affects their own good and their own personal profit, they would do that which should undo more doing — they would do something that would prevent King Polixenes from further doing my wife. Yes, and you, King Polixenes' cupbearer — whom I from a meaner position in life have raised to a high position and a seat among the powerful — you, who may see as plainly as Heaven sees Earth and Earth sees Heaven, how I am galled — you might 'spice' a cup with poison so that my enemy will have an everlasting sleep. Such a poisoned draught for him would be a medicine for me."

"Sir, my lord," Camillo said, "I could do this, and with no quick-acting potion. I could add to his drink a slow-acting dram that would not work quickly and obviously like many poisons would, but I cannot believe this crack — this sin of adultery — to be in my highly respected mistress, she who has always been so honorable. I have loved you —"

King Leontes interrupted, "If you don't believe me, then go rot! Do you think that I am so confused, so unsettled, that I would put myself in this vexing situation without good reason? Would I sully the purity and whiteness of my marriage sheets? To preserve their purity and whiteness leads to healthful and soothing sleep. But to spot their purity and whiteness leads to goads, thorns, nettles, tails of wasps! Would I bring scandal to the blood of the Prince my son, and make people wonder if he is legitimate? I think the Prince my son is legitimate and mine, and I love him as mine. Would I put myself in this vexing situation without good reason? Could any man so delude himself and turn away from reason and a loved one?"

"I must believe you, sir," Camillo said. "I do believe you; and I will fetch off — remove — the King of Bohemia because of it."

Camillo was perhaps being deliberately ambiguous. To "remove" the King of Bohemia could mean to kill him, or to send him safely away.

Camillo continued, "I will fetch off — remove — the King of Bohemia provided that, when he's removed, your Highness will take again your Queen as yours as you did at first. Do it for your son's sake; by doing so you will seal up and prevent gossiping tongues from doing you injury in courts and Kingdoms that are known and allied to yours."

"You advise me to do what I have already decided to do," King Leontes said. "I'll give no blemish to her honor — none at all."

"My lord, go then, and with a countenance as clear as friends have at feasts, be with the King of Bohemia and with your Queen. Pretend to be friendly to him. I am the King of Bohemia's cupbearer, and if he receives a wholesome and healthy beverage from me, then do not believe that I am your loyal servant."

"This is all that I have to say," King Leontes said. "If you kill King Polixenes, you will have one half of my heart. If you do not kill King Polixenes, you will split your own heart in two."

"I will do it, my lord," Camillo said.

"I will seem friendly, as you have advised me to be," King Leontes said.

He exited.

"Oh, miserable lady!" Camillo said. "But, as for me, what is my situation? I must be the poisoner of good King Polixenes. My reason for killing him is that I am obedient to my King, a King who is in rebellion against his true self and so will have all his followers also rebel against their true selves. If I do this deed, I will supposedly be rewarded — promotion supposedly follows the doing of this deed. Even if I could find thousands of examples of people who had killed anointed Kings and then flourished afterward, I would not do it; but since documents of brass or stone or parchment present not even one example of good things happening to the murderer of a King, then villainy — evil — itself ought to refuse to do such an evil act. I must leave King Leontes' court. Whether I kill King Polixenes, or I don't kill King Polixenes, bad things are certain to happen to me if I stay here."

He saw King Polixenes walking toward him and said, "My happy star, may you reign now! May I have good luck! Here comes the King of Bohemia."

King Polixenes said to himself, "This is strange. I think that my popularity here begins to wane. I met King Leontes, and he did not speak to me. Why?"

He then said out loud, "Good day, Camillo."

"Hail, most royal sir!"

"What is the news in the court?"

"Nothing unusual, my lord."

"King Leontes looks as he had lost some province — a region that he loves as he loves himself. Just now I met him with my customary compliment and greeting to him, but he hurriedly turned his eyes away from me and with a contemptuous sneer on his lips sped away from me and so he left me to consider what is happening that makes him change how he treats me."

"I dare not know, my lord," Camillo replied.

"What! Dare not! Or do not? Do you know, and dare not? Tell me what you know. You must know something. What you do know, you must know. If you cannot say something, it must be the case that you dare not say something. Good Camillo, your changed facial expression is like a mirror to me — my facial expression is also changing because of the changing way that King Leontes treats me. I must be somehow involved in what is happening because of how it is affecting me."

"A sickness is giving some of us distemper, but I cannot name the disease; and you are spreading the disease although you are healthy."

"What! I am spreading the disease! Do not think that I have the deadly look of the basilisk, the snake that is so poisonous that it kills the person who merely looks at it. I have looked on thousands of people, who have prospered by my looking on them, but I have killed none by looking at him. I am a benevolent King, not a malevolent tyrant.

"Camillo — as you are certainly a gentleman, and educated as a scholar; education no less adorns our good social position than our parents' noble names, by descent from whom we are gentlemen — please, if you know anything which I ought to know, do not conceal it and keep me in ignorance."

"I may not answer your appeal," Camillo said.

"A sickness caught from me, and yet I am well!" King Polixenes said. "My appeal must be answered. Listen to me, Camillo. I urge you, by all the parts of Mankind that honor acknowledges, whereof the least is not this appeal of mine, that you declare what probability of harm toward me you think may be coming.

Tell me how far off or how near the harm is. Tell me how to prevent the harm, if that is possible. If that is not possible, then tell me how best I can bear it."

"Sir, I will tell you," Camillo said, "since you, whom I think to be honorable, have made an appeal to my honor. Therefore, listen to my counsel, which must be as swiftly followed as I mean to utter it, or both yourself and I will cry out that we are lost, and that will be good night to our lives!"

"Speak on, good Camillo."

"I have been ordered by him to murder you."

"By whom, Camillo?"

"By King Leontes."

"For what reason?"

"He thinks — no, with all confidence he swears, as if he had seen it or had himself encouraged you to commit this vice — that you have touched his Queen in a way that is forbidden."

"Oh, if I have ever committed adultery with Queen Hermione, then may my royal blood turn into diseased jelly and may my name be yoked with Judas, who betrayed the Best — Jesus! May my freshest reputation turn into a stench that strikes the dullest nostril wherever I arrive, and may my approach be shunned — hated, too — worse than the greatest disease that anyone ever heard or read about!"

"You can try to deny his accusation by swearing by each individual star in Heaven and by all their astrological influences, but you will be as successful at forbidding the sea to obey the Moon as you will be using either sworn oaths of innocence or serious arguments to keep King Leontes from believing his foolish belief that you and his Queen have committed adultery. He believes strongly in this foolishness and will continue to believe it as long as his body is standing and he is alive."

"How did this belief come into existence and grow?" King Polixenes asked.

"I don't know," Camillo replied, "but I am sure that it is safer to avoid what is grown than to question how it was born. If therefore you dare to trust my honesty that lies enclosed in this trunk of mine that you shall take away with you as a pledge of my good faith, then let us leave tonight! I will whisper to your followers and inform them about this business, and I will by twos and threes at several back gates get them away from the city.

"As for myself, I'll put my fortunes at your service. I have no good future here because of what I have told you. Believe that what I have told you is true. I swear by the honor of my parents that I have said the truth. If you try to get evidence that what I have said is true, I dare not stand by. I will be in danger if I stay here. You yourself shall be no safer than a man who has been condemned by the King's own mouth, which has ordered you to be executed."

"I believe what you have told me," King Polixenes said. "I saw King Leontes' heart in his face. Give me your hand. Be my pilot and guide me, and your place shall be at my side. My ships are ready; my people expected me to leave here two days ago.

"King Leontes' jealousy is for a precious creature. Because Queen Hermione is splendid and rare, his jealousy must be great. Because his person and position are mighty, his jealousy must be violent. And because he believes that a man who has always professed friendship to him has dishonored him, why, his revenges must be bitterer.

"Fear casts a shadow over me. May a speedy departure be my friend, and may only comfort come to Queen Hermione from King Leontes and none of his ill-taken suspicion!

"Come, Camillo. I will respect you as a father if you save my life by carrying it away from here. Let us leave."

"I have the authority to order all the posterns to lock or unlock gates," Camillo said. "May it please your Highness to leave immediately and urgently. Come, sir, let us go."

CHAPTER 2

— 2.1 —

In a room in King Leontes' palace, Queen Hermione; her son, Mamillius; and some ladies were present.

Playfully, Queen Hermione said to the first lady, "Take the boy. He so pesters me that I can't endure it."

The first lady said to Mamillius, "Come, my gracious lord, shall I be your playfellow?"

"No, I'll have nothing to do with you."

"Why not, my sweet lord?"

"You'll kiss me hard and speak to me as if I were still a baby," he replied.

He then said to the second lady, "I love you better than I love her."

"Why, my lord?" she asked.

"Not because your brows are blacker," he said, "yet black brows, they say, become some women best, as long as there is not too much hair there, but only a semicircle or a half-Moon made with a pen."

"Who taught you this?" the second lady asked.

"I learnt it from women's faces," Mamillius replied. "Please, tell me what color are your eyebrows?"

The first lady replied, "Blue, my lord."

"No, that's a joke," Mamillius said. "I have seen a lady who had a blue nose, but not blue eyebrows."

"Listen," the first lady said. "The belly of the Queen your mother grows round quickly. She is pregnant, and we ladies shall soon present our services to a fine new boy or girl one of these days; and then you will want to play with us, if we will let you."

The second lady said, "The Queen's belly has grown recently into a good size. May the childbirth go well!"

"What are you talking about?" Hermione asked the ladies.

She then said to her son, "Come, sir, I am ready now for you again. Please, sit by me and tell me a tale."

"Shall the tale be merry or sad?" Mamillius asked.

"As merry as you want," Hermione replied.

"A sad tale's best for winter. I have a tale about ghosts and goblins."

"Let's hear that, good sir," Hermione said. "Come on, sit down. Come on, and do your best to frighten me with your ghosts. You're good at it."

"There was once a man —"

Hermione said to Mamillius, "Come, sit down; then go on with your story."

"He dwelt by a churchyard. I will tell it softly; yonder crickets shall not hear it."

The "crickets" were the ladies, who were chirping — talking — among themselves.

"Come on, then," Hermione said, "and whisper it in my ear."

King Leontes entered the room. With him were his advisor Antigonus, some other lords, and some attendants.

"Was King Polixenes seen there?" King Leontes asked. "Was his entourage? Was Camillo with him?"

The first lord said, "I saw them behind the grove of pines; never have I seen men hurry so on their way. I watched them until they reached their ships."

"How blessed am I in my just censure, in my true opinion!" King Leontes said. "All my suspicions are justified. But I wish that I had lesser knowledge! How accursed I am by being so blessed with knowledge! I would be much happier if I did not know what I know.

"A spider may be steeped in a cup, and one may drink, depart, and yet suffer from no venom, for the drinker's knowledge is not infected, but if one should show the spider to the drinker and make known to him what he has drunk, then the drinker vomits, and his sides heave violently.

"I have drunk, and I have seen the spider.

"Camillo was King Polixenes' accomplice in this; he was his pander. There is a plot against my life and my crown. All's true that I mistrusted — all that I suspected is true. That false villain — Camillo! — whom I employed was pre-employed by King Polixenes. Camillo has revealed to King Polixenes what I learned, and I remain a tortured thing. Yes, I am a counter in a game for them to manipulate at will.

"How is it that the back gates were opened to them so easily?"

"They opened because of Camillo's great authority," the first lord said. "They open at Camillo's orders no less than at your orders."

"I know that to be true only too well," King Leontes replied.

He said to Queen Hermione, "Give me the boy, our son. I am glad you did not breastfeed him. Although he bears some signs of me, yet you have too much blood in him."

"What is this?" Hermione asked. "Some kind of game or joke?"

"Take the boy away," King Leontes ordered. "He shall not come into her presence. Take him away! Let her entertain herself with the child that is now swelling her belly."

He said to Queen Hermione, "King Polixenes has made your belly swell up like this."

Thinking still that this must be some kind of game or joke, Hermione replied, "But I say that he did not, and I will be sworn that you will believe what I say, no matter how much you might be leaning to the wrong belief."

Swearing and saying are different. Hermione at this time believed that if she merely said something without swearing to it that her husband would believe her.

King Leontes said, "My lords, look at her. Look at her carefully. If you were to be about to say, 'She is a good lady,' the justice of your hearts would add, 'It is a pity she is not honest and honorable.'

"Praise her only for her exterior form and beauty, which truly deserve high praise, and immediately will come the shrug, the hum, aka hmm, or ha, these hints of deficiency that the voice of defamation uses — oh, I am mistaken because I should have said that the voice of mercy uses because the voice of defamation will sear virtue itself. Mercy requires you to use these shrugs, these hums and ha's, after you say, 'She's beautiful,' but before you can say, 'She's honest and chaste.' Mercy does not want to say the truth openly and clearly. But let it be known from the man who has the most reason to grieve the truth — Queen Hermione is an adulteress."

"Should a villain say that I am an adulteress," Hermione said, "even if he were the most complete villain in the world, his saying this would make him twice the villain he was. You, my lord, are mistaken."

"You are mistaken," King Leontes replied. "My lady, you have mistaken King Polixenes for King Leontes! You thing! I will not call a creature of your place the word that you ought to be called —"

He thought, *Whore!*

"— lest uncivilized people, making me the precedent, should use such language to refer to people of all social classes and neglect to make a civilized distinction between a Prince and a beggar."

He said to the other adults in the room, "I have said that she's an adulteress. I have said with whom. In addition, she's a traitor and Camillo is her accomplice. Camillo is a man who knows what she ought to be ashamed of, even if it were known only by her most vile principal, King Polixenes — she's a bed-swerver and adulteress. She is even as bad as those whom vulgar people give the nastiest names, yes, and she knew in advance about King Polixenes' and Camillo's recent escape from me."

"No, I swear by my life," Hermione said, "I know nothing about any of this. After you have come to clearer and true knowledge, you will be grieved because you have thus accused me in public! My good lord, when you say then that you were mistaken now, it shall scarcely fully make up for this accusation."

"You are wrong that I am mistaken," King Leontes said. "If I am mistaken in those foundations that I build upon, then the entire Earth is not big enough to bear the weight of a schoolboy's toy top."

He said to his attendants, "Take her away! Take her to prison! Anyone who will speak up for her is himself implicitly guilty because he is speaking up for her."

"Some ill planet is reigning now and casting bad astrological influences," Hermione said. "I must be patient until the Heavens look at me more favorably.

"My good lords, I am not prone to weeping, as women commonly are. The lack of such useless dew perhaps shall make you lack pity for me, but I have lodged here in my heart honorable grief that burns worse than tears drown. I ask you all, my lords, to judge me as your benevolent tendencies shall best instruct you. Now let the King's will be performed!"

No one had moved to take Hermione to prison because no one believed that she was guilty of adultery and everyone was impressed by her dignity.

King Leontes asked, "Shall I be obeyed?"

"Who is it who goes with me?" Hermione asked. She was soon to give birth, and so she needed attendants to take care of her.

She asked her husband, "Please, your Highness, allow my women attendants to be with me; for as you can see my plight requires it."

She said to her servants, "Do not weep, good fools; there is no cause for weeping. If you should know that your mistress has ever deserved prison, then you may abound in tears as the truth about me comes out. But right now this imprisonment I go to is for my better grace. I shall gain spiritual rewards by suffering."

"*Adieu*, my lord. I never wished to see you sorry; now I trust I shall.

"My women, come; you have permission to go with me."

King Leontes ordered his attendants, "Go, do our bidding; take her away!"

Hermione, guarded, exited with her female attendants.

The first lord said, "I beg your Highness, call the Queen back again."

Antigonus, a lord and advisor who was married to Paulina, one of Queen Hermione's confidants, said to King Leontes, "Be certain that you are doing the right thing, sir, lest your justice result in violence, in which case three great ones will suffer: yourself, your Queen, and your son."

The first lord said, "For Queen Hermione, my lord, I dare to lay my life down and I will do it, sir, if it pleases you to accept it. I swear that the Queen is spotless in the eyes of Heaven and to you — I mean that she is innocent of this adultery that you accuse her of."

Antigonus said, "If it should be proved that Queen Hermione is guilty of adultery, I will watch where I lodge my wife — as I keep my mares away from stallions, I will keep my wife away from men. I'll go about with a leash tied to her so that I can keep an eye on her. I will trust her no farther than I can feel and see her because every inch of every woman in the world — indeed, every gram of every woman's flesh — is false, if Queen Hermione is false and an adulteress."

"Be quiet, everyone!" King Leontes ordered.

The first lord began, "My good lord —"

Antigonus interrupted and said to King Leontes, "It is for you we speak, not for ourselves. Some manipulator who will be damned for misleading you has abused you. I wish that I knew who the villain is — I would make his life on Earth a living Hell!

"If Queen Hermione is honor-flawed, I know what I will do. I have three daughters; the eldest is eleven years old, and the second and the third are nine and about five years old. If it is true that Queen Hermione is an adulteress, they'll pay for it, I swear. I'll sterilize all my daughters. By age fourteen, they shall not be able to give birth to bastards. My daughters are co-heirs; I have no sons and so my daughters will inherit and share my possessions. I would rather sterilize myself and remove all chance of my ever having sons than to allow my daughters to give birth to bastards."

"Stop talking," King Leontes ordered Antigonus. "I want to hear no more. You smell this business with a sense as cold as a dead man's nose, but I see it and feel it as you feel me doing this" — here King Leontes grabbed and pulled Antigonus' beard — "and as you see my fingers."

Antigonus replied, "If it is true that Queen Hermione is an adulteress, we need no grave in which to bury honesty and chasteness because there's not a grain of it left to sweeten the face of the whole dungy earth."

"What!" King Leontes said. "You do not believe me! Do I lack credit?"

The first lord said, "I swear upon this ground that I would prefer that you lacked credit than I, my lord. You say that Queen Hermione is guilty; I say that she is innocent. It would please me better to have her honor proved true than your suspicion, no matter how you might be blamed for being wrong."

Using the royal plural, King Leontes replied, "Why, what need have we to debate with you about this? We will instead follow our own powerful feelings. Our prerogative has not been to ask you for your advice; instead, our natural goodness has given you information and facts. If you lack or pretend to lack the intelligence to understand what we have told you — if you cannot or will not admit that this is true, as we have done — then know that we need no more of your advice. The matter, the loss, the gain, and the ordering of it are all properly our own business."

"And I wish, my liege," Antigonus said, "that you had kept quiet and only in your silent judgment had worked out the problem, without making it public."

"How could that be?" King Leontes said. "Either you are very ignorant because of your age, or you were born a fool. Camillo's flight, added to the intimacy in public between King Polixenes and Hermione, which was so shameless and obvious that it gave rise to great suspicion of adultery — a suspicion that lacked only seeing them actually commit adultery — along with all the other evidence, show that I am right and that we must take action.

"Yet, for a greater confirmation, because in an act of this importance it would be a shame to be rash, I have sent to sacred Delphos, to Apollo's temple, Cleomenes and Dion, whom you know to have more than adequate competence. They will consult the oracle of Delphos, who is known to tell the truth, and they will bring back the words of the oracle. The spiritual counsel of the oracle will be revealed, and it shall either stop or spur me. Have I done well?"

Delphos is a name for Delos, the island where the god Apollo was born.

The first lord approved of this action: "Well done, my lord."

"Though I am satisfied that I know the truth and I do not need more than what I know," King Leontes said, "yet the oracle shall give rest to the minds of other people, such as that man whose ignorant credulity will not believe the truth."

He was speaking in particular about Antigonus.

King Leontes added, "We have thought it good that Hermione shall be confined away from our presence lest that the treachery of the two fled from here — King Polixenes and Camillo, who planned to murder me — be performed by her.

"Come, follow us; we will speak in public. This business will cause everyone concern. It will arouse everyone."

Antigonus thought, *It will arouse everyone to laughter, I believe, if the good truth were known. It is ridiculous to think that Queen Hermione has committed adultery.*

Paulina was visiting the prison in which Queen Hermione was kept. She was trying to see her and talk to her. Accompanying her were a gentleman and some female attendants.

Paulina said to the gentleman, "Call the jailer to come to me; tell him who I am."

Paulina's husband was Lord Antigonus; her rank was high in Sicily.

The gentleman exited to carry out the errand, and Paulina said to herself about Queen Hermione, "Good lady, no court in Europe is too good for you, so why are you in prison?"

The gentleman came back with the jailer.

Paulina said to the jailer, "Now, good sir, you know who I am, don't you?"

"I know that you are a worthy lady and one whom I much respect," the jailer replied.

"Then please take me to Queen Hermione."

"I cannot, madam," the jailer replied. "King Leontes has given explicit orders that prevent me from doing that."

"Here's a lot of ado," Paulina said. "You lock up honesty and honor from the access of noble visitors!"

She said sarcastically, "Is it lawful, do you think, for me to see her female attendants? Can I see any of them? Can I see Emilia?"

"Madam," the jailer said, "if you will order your attendants to leave, I shall bring Emilia here."

"Please, bring her here," Paulina said to the jailer.

To her attendants, she said, "Please go into another room."

Her female attendants and the gentleman left.

The jailer added, "Madam, I must be present during your conversation with Emilia."

"Well, so be it," Paulina replied.

The jailer departed, and Paulina said to herself, "Here's such ado to make no stain a stain that cannot covered up with a dye job. Queen Hermione has committed no sin and yet people are going to a lot of trouble to make it seem that she has committed a sin that cannot be concealed."

The jailer returned with Emilia.

Paulina asked Emilia, "Dear gentlewoman, how is our gracious Queen Hermione doing?"

"She is doing as well as one so great and so forlorn can bear up. Because of her frights and griefs, which are greater than any tender lady has ever borne, she has given birth prematurely."

"To a boy?" Paulina asked.

"A daughter, and a good, healthy baby; she is vigorous and likely to live. The Queen receives much comfort from her daughter, and she says, 'My poor prisoner, I am as innocent as you.'"

"I agree," Paulina said. "Queen Hermione is as innocent as a newborn babe. Curse these dangerous unsafe fits of lunacy in King Leontes! He must be told about the birth of his daughter, and he shall. A woman should tell him, and I will take the job upon me. I will tell the truth and not flatter the King. If I prove honey-mouthed and flatter the King, let my tongue blister from the lies I tell. Also, let my tongue never again be the trumpeter to my red-faced anger."

In this society, a herald, dressed in red, sometimes bore an angry message. A trumpeter would precede the herald. Paulina planned to bear an angry message to King Leontes; she would be red-faced because of her anger, and her tongue would trumpet her angry message.

Paulina added, "Please, Emilia, present my compliments to the Queen. If she dares trust me with her little babe, I'll show it to the King and undertake to be her loudest, most vigilant advocate. We do not know how he may soften at the sight of the child. The silence of pure innocence often persuades when speaking fails."

Emilia replied, "Most worthy madam, your honor and your goodness are so evident that this your voluntary undertaking cannot miss having a successful result. No other lady living is so suitable to undertake this mission. If it will please your ladyship to wait in the next room, I'll immediately tell the Queen of your most noble offer. Just today she vigorously debated whether to implement this same plan you are advocating, but she dared not ask any worthy official to carry it out because she was afraid that they would refuse to do so."

"Tell her, Emilia," Paulina said, "that I'll use the tongue I have in the Queen's behalf. If words of wisdom flow from it the way that courage and boldness will flow from my heart, let no one doubt that I shall do good."

"May you be blest for it!" Emilia said. "I'll go to the Queen. Please, come a little nearer."

The jailer, who was concerned that King Leontes could punish him, said to Paulina, "Madam, if it pleases the Queen to send the babe, I do not know what will happen to me if I allow the babe to leave the prison. I do not have an order to allow the babe to leave."

"You need not fear anything, sir," Paulina said. "This child was a prisoner in the Queen's womb and is by the lawful process of great nature freed from it and therefore is a free being. The babe is not a party against whom the King is angry, and the babe is not guilty of — if the sin should exist — the sin of the Queen."

"I believe what you say," the jailer said.

"Do not be afraid," Paulina said. "I swear by my honor that I will stand between you and danger."

King Leontes was alone in a room in his palace.

He said to himself, "I cannot sleep either at night nor during the day. I am showing weakness — mere weakness — in this. If only the people who caused my distress were not still alive — well, if one of the causes of my distress were not still alive. The adulteress Queen Hermione is within my power, but the licentious King Polixenes is quite beyond the reach of my arm. He is out of range of any plot my brain can come up with, but I can hook her to me the way that grappling hooks can seize a ship at sea. If she were gone, given a death by being burned alive, I may be able to sleep a little again."

He heard a noise and asked, "Who's there?"

A servant entered the room and asked, "My lord?"

"How is my son?" King Leontes asked.

"He slept well last night; it is hoped that his sickness is over."

"This shows his nobleness!" King Leontes said. "Learning about the dishonor of his mother, he immediately declined, drooped, took it deeply, fastened and fixed the shame of it in himself; this harmed his spirit, affecting his appetite and his sleep, and he completely languished.

"Leave me alone. Go and see how he fares."

The servant exited.

"Damn! Damn!" King Leontes said. "Let me not think about King Polixenes. Thoughts about me getting revenge upon him end up hurting only myself. He is a very mighty King, and his supporters and his allies are also very mighty — so mighty that I cannot get revenge upon him. So I will let him be until a time may be right for me to get vengeance against him.

"But I can get vengeance against Queen Hermione right now. Camillo and King Polixenes are both laughing at me; they are entertained by my sorrow. They would not laugh if I could reach them, nor shall she — because she is within my power."

Paulina, carrying the daughter of King Leontes and Queen Hermione, entered the room. With her were Antigonus, some lords, and some attendants. Antigonus and the lords were trying — but failing — to prevent her from entering the room.

The first lord said, "You must not enter."

"My good lords," Paulina said, "instead of resisting me, be my supporters. Do you fear King Leontes' tyrannous passion more than you fear for Queen Hermione's life? She is a gracious and innocent soul; she is more free from sin than he is jealous."

Antigonus, her husband, said, "That's enough."

A servant said, "Madam, King Leontes has not slept tonight; he has commanded that no one should come and see him."

"Don't be so vehement, good sir," Paulina said. "I have come to bring King Leontes the ability to sleep. Such people as you who creep like shadows by him and pity every one of his needless and unnecessary sighs do him no good. It is such people as you who nourish the cause of his inability to sleep. I have come with words that are as medicinal as they are true; my words are honest and they will purge King Leontes of that mood that keeps him from sleeping."

"What is that noise?" King Leontes asked.

Coming closer to King Leontes, Paulina replied, "This is not noise, my lord; this is a necessary conference about getting some godparents for your Highness' daughter."

She showed King Leontes' infant daughter to him.

"What!" King Leontes said. "Take that audacious lady away! Antigonus, I ordered you to not allow her to come near me. I knew she would try to see me."

"I told her not to try to see you, my lord," Antigonus said. "I told her that if she tried to see you she would arouse both your displeasure and mine."

"What! Can't you make your wife obey your orders?" King Leontes asked.

"When he orders me to avoid all dishonesty, he can," Paulina said. "In this business, however, he cannot make me obey his orders unless he takes the course that you have done with your own wife — commit me to prison because I have committed an honorable action."

"You heard her," Antigonus said to King Leontes, "When she takes the reins and thereby takes control, I let her run, but she will not stumble."

He meant that he gave his wife much freedom, but his wife acted correctly. In fact, his wife was acting ethically by ignoring his and the King's orders and insisting on talking to the King.

"My good liege," Paulina said, "I have come to you. I beg that you listen to me — your loyal servant, your physician, and your most obedient counselor

— yet I am the person who dares to appear less than those things in your eyes because I will not approve of your evils, unlike most of the people who only appear to be loyal to you and only appear to serve you well. I say to you that I have come from your good Queen."

"Good Queen!" King Leontes said.

"Good Queen, my lord," Paulina repeated. "Good Queen; I say good Queen. If I were a man, I would prove her innocence with a trial by combat, even if I were the most menial and the weakest man around you."

In a trial by combat, two men fought. Because this society believed that God would protect the person who was in the right, the winner was in the right. If the winner had been accused, by winning the combat, the winner showed that he was innocent. If the winner had done the accusing, by winning the combat, the winner showed that his accusations were true.

"Force her to leave," King Leontes ordered.

"Let the man who regards his eyes as mere trifles be the first to lay hands on me," Paulina said. "I will leave under my own power, but only after I have finished my business here. The good Queen, and yes, she is good, has given birth to your daughter. Here she is; your Queen commends this girl to your blessing."

Paulina lay the infant Princess on the floor.

"Out!" King Leontes ordered. "You are a mannish witch! Take her away! Throw her out the door! She is a bawd who keeps the secrets of those illicit lovers for whom she is the go-between!"

"That is not true," Paulina said. "I am as ignorant of such an occupation as you are when you call me a bawd, and I am no less honest and chaste than you are mad. That is enough, I say, as this world goes, for me to be regarded as honest and chaste."

"Traitors!" King Leontes shouted. "Won't you push her out of the room? Give her the bastard."

He shouted at Antigonus, "You dotard! You are hen-pecked. Your dame Partlet has shoved you from your roost. Pick up the bastard. Pick it up, I say, and give it to your crone."

"Dame Partlet" was a traditional name for a hen.

Paulina said to her husband, "Your hands will be forever despised if you pick up the Princess and so acknowledge that false and base name of 'bastard' that King Leontes has unjustly given to her!"

King Leontes said about Antigonus, "He is afraid of his wife."

"I wish that you were afraid of your wife," Paulina replied. "If you were, you would acknowledge that your children really are your children."

"This is a nest of traitors!" King Leontes shouted.

"I am not a traitor," Antigonus said. "I swear it by the Sun."

"And I am not a traitor," Paulina said, "nor is any man here except one, and that man is the King himself because he is betraying and slandering the sacred honor of himself, his Queen, his son who hopes to become King one day, and his infant daughter. Slander has a sting that is sharper than the sword's. King Leontes will not remove the root of his opinion, which is as rotten as ever oak or stone was sound. As the case now stands, slander is a curse that he cannot be compelled to remove. As King, Leontes is above the law; if he were not King, Hermione could seek justice in a court of law."

"She is a nag and a scold who recently beat her husband and now torments me!" King Leontes said. "This brat is no child of mine; it is the child of King Polixenes. Take it away, and together with its dam — Queen Hermione — throw it into fire!"

"This child is yours," Paulina said. "And, if I may lay the old proverb to your charge, it is all the worse for looking like you.

"Behold, my lords, this infant girl. She is a copy of her father. Although the print is little, the whole matter and copy of the father — his eye, nose, lip, the way he wrinkles his forehead, the cleft in his chin and the pretty dimples in his cheeks, his smiles, the very mold and frame of his hands, fingernails, and fingers — can be found in her.

"Good goddess Nature, you who have made this infant resemble so much her father, if you have the ordering of her mind, too, do not give her jealousy, lest she suspect, as he does, that her future children will not be her husband's!

"King Leontes' jealousy is silly. How silly is it? It is as silly as a jealous woman who has always been faithful to her husband but who is nevertheless afraid that her husband's infidelity may cause the children to whom she has given birth to be illegitimate!"

King Leontes shouted, "You are a gross and rude hag and, you, Antigonus, you loser, you ought to be hanged because you will not make your wife shut up."

"If you hang all the husbands who cannot make their wives shut up, you'll find yourself with hardly one subject," Antigonus replied.

"Once more, take her away," King Leontes ordered.

"A most unworthy and unnatural lord can do no more evil than you have done," Paulina said.

"I'll have you burnt to death," King Leontes said.

"I don't care," Paulina said. "If you have me burnt to death, the heretic will be the person who causes the fire to be made, not the woman who burns in it. I will not call you a tyrant, but this most cruel treatment of your Queen, with you unable to produce any evidence against her except your own weak-hinged imagination, stinks somewhat of tyranny and will make your reputation in the world ignoble and scandalous."

"By the oaths of loyalty that you have sworn to me," King Leontes said, "I order you to throw this woman out of my chamber! If I were a tyrant, would she still be alive? If I were a tyrant, she would not dare to call me a tyrant. Throw her out!"

Finally, some lords approached Paulina to physically throw her out.

"Please, do not push me," Paulina said. "I am leaving. Look after your baby, my lord; it is your legitimate offspring. May Jove send her a better guiding spirit than you! Why are you lords using your hands to throw me out? You lords who ignore the King's foolish behavior will never do him any good — not one of you. And so farewell; we are gone."

She departed. A couple of lords followed her to make sure that she was really leaving.

King Leontes said to Antigonus, "You, traitor, have set on your wife to do this. This is my child, she said? Take it away! You, Antigonus, who have a heart that pities it, take it away and see that it is immediately thrown into a fire and burnt up. You, Antigonus, and only you do this. Do this immediately, and within this hour bring me word that it has been done, and bring me evidence — good testimony — that it has been done, or I'll seize your life and all the property that you call your own. If you refuse to obey my order and want to encounter and suffer my wrath, say so. The bastard's brains with these my own hands I shall dash out. Go, take it and throw it in the fire because you are the one who made your wife, Paulina, do this."

"I did not do that, sir," Antigonus said. "These lords, my noble fellows, if they please, can testify that I am innocent of that charge."

A lord said, "We can."

Another lord said, "My royal liege, Antigonus is not guilty of Paulina's coming here.

"All of you are liars," King Leontes said.

A lord replied, "Please, your Highness, give us better credit than that. We have always truly served you, and we beg you to acknowledge that, and on our knees we beg, as recompense of our valuable services to you both in the past and to come, that you change your mind about throwing this infant into the fire. That deed is so horrible and so bloody that it must lead on to some foul result. We all kneel before you."

"Each wind that blows treats me like a feather," King Leontes said. "Shall I live on to see this bastard kneel before me and call me father? It is better to burn it now than to curse it then. But so be it; let it live."

He instantly changed his mind and said, "No, it shall not live."

He then said, "You, sir, Antigonus, come here. You have been so tenderly officious along with your wife, Paulina — or should I call her Lady Margery Hen, your midwife there — to save this bastard's life. Yes, it is a bastard. I am as sure of that as I am that your beard is grey. What will you do to save this brat's life?"

"Anything, my lord, that I have the ability to do and that is honorable. I will do at least this much — I will pawn the little blood and few years that I have left to save this innocent baby. I will do anything that is possible."

"What I ask you to do shall be possible," King Leontes said. "Swear by the cross-piece of this sword that you will perform my bidding."

"I will swear, my lord."

"Listen carefully and do what we tell you to do," King Leontes said, using the royal plural. "If you fail to do exactly what we tell you to do, the result shall not only be death to yourself but to your lewd-tongued wife, whom for now we pardon. We order you, who have sworn to obey us, to carry this female bastard away from here and bear it to some remote and deserted place quite out of our dominions, and that you leave it there, without any more mercy. Let it protect itself; let it be exposed to wild animals and the weather. As by strange — unusual and foreign — fortune this baby came to us, I do justly order you, on your soul's peril — if you break your oath, your soul will be sent to Hell — and your body's torture, to leave it in some foreign place where fortune and luck shall either bring it aid or death. Pick up the infant."

Antigonus picked up the baby girl and said, "I swear to do this, although an immediate death would have been more merciful for the baby.

"Come on, poor babe. I hope that some powerful spirit will instruct the hawks and ravens to be your caretakers! Wolves and bears, they say, have cast aside their savageness and done such offices of pity."

Antigonus was thinking of such stories as that of a she-wolf suckling the infants Romulus and Remus, who founded the city of Rome. He may have also been thinking of 1 Kings 17:6: "*And the ravens brought him [the prophet Elijah] bread and flesh in the morning, and bread and flesh in the evening; and he drank of the brook.*"

Antigonus then said to King Leontes, "Sir, I hope that you are more prosperous than you deserve to be because of this deed!"

He then said to the baby girl, "And may Heaven send mercy to fight on your side against this cruelty. Poor thing, you are condemned to die!"

Antigonus departed, carrying the baby girl.

King Leontes said, "No, I'll not rear the child of another man."

A servant entered the room and said, "If it please your Highness, an hour ago messages came from the men whom you sent to the oracle. Cleomenes and Dion have safely arrived from Delphos. Both of them have landed on our country's shore, and they are hurrying to your court."

A lord said, "If it please you, sir, their speed has been unprecedented."

"They have been absent twenty-three days," King Leontes said. "They made good speed. This is evidence that the great god Apollo wants the truth about my wife to be known quickly.

"Prepare yourselves, lords. Summon a session of court so that we may arraign our most disloyal lady. She has been publicly accused, and so she shall have a just and open trial. As long as she lives, my heart will be a burden to me.

"Leave me, and do what I have ordered you to do."

CHAPTER 3

— 3.1 —

Outside an inn in Sicily, Cleomenes and Dion were talking.

Cleomenes said about Delphos, which was sacred to the god Apollo, whose birthplace it was, "The climate is delightful, the air most sweet, the island fertile, and the temple much surpassing the usual praise said about it."

Dion replied, "I shall talk about, because they are what most impressed me, the celestial vestments — that is the name that I think I should use to describe them — and the reverence of the serious people who wore them. And, oh, the sacrifice! How ceremonious, solemn, and unearthly it was in the offering!"

"But out of everything, the blast of thunder and the ear-deafening voice of the oracle, which was like the thunder of Jove, so overwhelmed my senses that I was nothing," Cleomenes said.

"If the result of the journey prove as successful to the Queen — I hope that it will be so! — as it has been to us rare, pleasant, speedy, the time it took to make the journey is very well spent."

Cleomenes said, "May great Apollo make everything turn out for the best! I do not like these proclamations we have seen that cast aspersions on Queen Hermione and accuse her of serious crimes and sins."

"Our violently speedy journey and carrying of the oracle written by the priest at Delphos will either clear Queen Hermione's name by pronouncing her innocent or end this business by pronouncing her guilty. Inspired by the god Apollo, his priest knows whether Queen Hermione is innocent or guilty. Apollo's great divine sealed up the oracle — the god's words — and when those words are read, something remarkable will become known. Let's go! We have fresh horses! May the outcome of our journey be good and gracious!"

In a court of justice were King Leontes and some lords and officers.

King Leontes said, using the royal plural, "Let this trial begin, although it causes us great grief and strikes right at our heart. The defendant is the daughter of a King, our wife, and one too much beloved by us. Let this trial clear us of the charge of being tyrannous, since we so openly proceed in justice, which shall have due course, whether the trial ends with the defendant being pronounced guilty or ends with the defendant being pronounced innocent.

"Produce the prisoner."

An officer said, "It is his Highness' pleasure that the Queen appear in person here in this court. Silence!"

Queen Hermione, her guards, Paulina, and some female attendants entered the courtroom.

King Leontes ordered, "Read the indictment."

The officer read, "Hermione, Queen to the worthy Leontes, King of Sicily, you are here accused and arraigned of high treason in committing adultery with Polixenes, King of Bohemia, and conspiring with Camillo to take away the life of our sovereign lord the King, your royal husband. When the murder plot was partly revealed by circumstances, you, Hermione, contrary to the faith and allegiance of a true subject, advised and aided the would-be assassins, for their safety, to flee by night."

Queen Hermione said, "Since what I will say must be only that which contradicts my accusation and since no one except me will testify on my behalf, it shall scarcely help me to say 'not guilty.' My integrity is already thought to be nonexistent, and so my plea of 'not guilty' will not be believed.

"But there is this: If divine powers see our human actions — and they do — I do not doubt but innocence shall make false accusation blush and patience make tyranny tremble.

"You, my lord the King, best know, although you will pretend not to know, that my past life has been as continent, as chaste, and as true as I am now unhappy. This is more than a play can equal, even if it is created and played in order to fascinate spectators. Look at me! I am a fellow of the royal bed, wife to the King. I own a share of the throne. I am a great King's daughter. I am the mother to a Prince who hopes to rule the Kingdom one day. Yet here I am standing so I can plead in vain for life and honor in front of anyone who wants to come and hear.

"As for life, I prize it as much as I prize grief, which I can do without. As for honor, it is a heritage that descends from me to my children, and I will fight for only that.

"I appeal to your own conscience, sir, King, before Polixenes came to your court. Remember how I was in your favor and how I deserved to be so. Since Polixenes came to visit you, what behavior so wrong have I committed that I am forced to appear now in court? If I have gone one jot beyond the boundary of honor, either in act or intention, may the hearts of all who hear me be hardened, and may my closest relatives cry 'Damn you!' as they stand by my grave!"

King Leontes said, "I have never heard yet of anyone who had the impudence to commit a bold sin but lacked the impudence to deny that he or she had committed that sin."

"That's true enough," Queen Hermione said, "although it is a saying, sir, that does not apply to my actions."

"You will not admit it," King Leontes said.

"I will not at all acknowledge sins other than the so-called 'sin' I am accused of. That is what I will talk about. Let me talk about Polixenes, with whom I am accused of committing adultery and treason. My friendship with him was such as he honorably deserved. I gave him the friendship that becomes a lady like me; that friendship was even such as you yourself wanted me to show him. I did not go beyond that kind of friendship, and if I had not shown that kind of friendship I think that I would have been showing both disobedience and ingratitude to you and to your friend, who had freely expressed his friendship for you ever since he could speak, from infancy.

"Now, as for the charge of conspiracy, I do not know how it tastes; and I would not even if it were dished on a plate so I could taste it. I know nothing about conspiracy. All I know of the charge of conspiracy is that Camillo was an honest man. As for why he left your court, the gods themselves, if they know no more than I do, are ignorant."

King Leontes said, "You knew of his departure, as you know what you have undertaken to do in his absence."

King Leontes was accusing his wife of planning to murder him following the flight of Camillo and King Polixenes.

"Sir, you speak a language that I do not understand," Queen Hermione said. "My life is being targeted by your dreams, and I will lay my life down."

"Your actions are my dreams," King Leontes said sarcastically. "You had a bastard by Polixenes, and I only dreamed it. As you were past all shame — those who are guilty of your crime are past all shame — so you are past all truth. Denying this will hurt you more than help you. Just like your brat has been cast out, left by itself, with no father owning it — which is, indeed, a criminal act that you are more responsible for than it — so you shall feel our justice, whose easiest punishment will be no less than death."

A harder punishment would be to have her tortured and then killed.

"Sir, spare your threats," Queen Hermione said with dignity. "The bugbear — death — that you would frighten me with is something that I seek. To me life can be no profitable existence. The crown and comfort of my life — your favor — I give up as lost; for I feel that they are gone, although I do not know how they vanished.

"My second joy is my son, the first-fruits of my body, but I am barred from his presence as if I were infected with a contagious disease.

"My third comfort is my daughter, who was born under a very unlucky star. She has been taken from my breast, with the innocent milk in its most innocent mouth, so it can be murdered.

"I myself am proclaimed to be a strumpet on proclamations that have been displayed on every post. With immodest hatred, people have denied me a period of rest following childbirth, which is a privilege that belongs to women of every social class. Finally, I have been rushed to this place, in the open air, before I have gotten my strength back following childbirth."

In their society, fresh air was regarded as unhealthy for invalids.

Queen Hermione continued, "Now, my liege, tell me what blessings I have here while I am alive that should make me fear to die? Therefore proceed. But yet hear one more thing: Do not misunderstand me. I do not value my life as much as I value a straw, but I do value my honor, which I want to be cleared. If I am judged guilty and condemned because of mere surmises, without any other evidence, I tell you that the judgment is tyranny and not law."

She said to the court, "Your honors, I submit myself to the oracle. Let Apollo be my judge!"

The first lord said, "Your request is entirely just. Therefore, officers, bring forth, and in Apollo's name, his oracle."

Some officers exited to get Cleomenes and Dion and the oracle that they had brought back from Delphos.

Queen Hermione said, "The Emperor of Russia was my father. I wish that he were alive, and here watching his daughter's trial! I wish that he could see the completeness of my misery with his eyes filled with pity, not revenge!"

The officers returned with Cleomenes and Dion.

An officer said, "You shall swear upon this sword of justice, that you, Cleomenes and Dion, have both been at Delphos, and from thence have brought back this sealed-up oracle, which was by the hand of great Apollo's priest delivered to you, and that, since then, you have not dared to break the holy seal nor read the secrets in it."

Cleomenes and Dion said, "All this we swear."

King Leontes said, "Break the seals of the oracle and read it out loud."

The officer read, "Hermione is chaste; Polixenes blameless; Camillo a true subject; Leontes a jealous tyrant; his innocent babe truly begotten and legitimate; and the King shall live without an heir, if that babe who is lost is not found."

The lords recited, "Now blessed be the great Apollo!"

Hermione said, "May Apollo be praised!"

King Leontes asked, "Have you read truthfully what is written in the oracle?"

The officer replied, "Yes, my lord; exactly as it is here set down."

King Leontes said, "There is no truth at all in the oracle. The trial shall proceed: This is mere falsehood."

By saying that, King Leontes committed blasphemy. He was calling the priest of Apollo a liar, and by extension he was calling the great god Apollo a liar. Insulted gods often quickly take vengeance.

An excited servant entered the courtroom and said, "My lord the King! The King!"

"What is the matter?" King Leontes asked.

The servant said, "Sir, I shall be hated for reporting this news! The Prince your son, through merely imagining and fearing what would happen to his mother the Queen, is gone."

"What do you mean? Gone?" King Leontes said.

"He is dead," the servant replied.

King Leontes repented immediately, saying, "Apollo is angry; and the Heavens themselves strike at my injustice."

Queen Hermione fainted.

King Leontes said, "What is happening there?"

Paulina replied, "This news is mortal to the Queen. Look down and see what death is doing to her."

"Take her away from here and care for her," King Leontes ordered. "Her heart is only over-stressed; she will recover. I have too much believed my own suspicions. Please, tenderly give her some remedies to help her."

Paulina and the ladies exited, carrying Queen Hermione.

King Leontes said, "Apollo, pardon my great profaneness against your oracle! I'll take steps to be reconciled with Polixenes, newly woo my Queen, and recall the good Camillo, whom I proclaim to be a man of truth and of mercy.

"When I was carried away by my jealousies and began to think bloody thoughts about revenge, I chose Camillo to be the person to poison my friend Polixenes. This would have been done, but the good mind of Camillo delayed implementing my command to quickly murder Polixenes, although I threatened him with death if he did not kill Polixenes and although I promised to reward him if he did kill Polixenes. Camillo, who is very humane and filled with honor, went to my Kingly guest and revealed my plot. He left his fortune and possessions, which you know are great, here, and he committed himself to the hazard of all uncertainties, with no riches other than his honor. How he glistens through my rust! And how his pity makes by contrast my deeds all the blacker!"

Paulina returned and said, "Grief and pain! Cut the tight laces of my bodice so that I can breathe, or my pounding heart will break the laces and break itself, too."

The first lord said, "What is wrong, good lady?"

Paulina said to King Leontes, "What well-thought-out torments, tyrant, do you have for me? What wheels upon which to break my body? Racks? Fires? What flaying — being skinned alive? Boiling, either in cauldrons filled with lead or in cauldrons filled with oil? What old or newer torture must I receive, whose every word deserves to suffer your very worst torture?

"Your tyranny working together with your jealousies — imaginings too weak for boys, and too simple-minded and silly for nine-year-old girls — think what your tyranny and jealousies have done and then run mad indeed, stark mad! Why? Because all your former foolish actions were but tastes of this new evil you have caused.

"That you betrayed Polixenes is nothing; that merely showed that you, a fool, are inconstant and damnably ungrateful. Nor did it count for much that you would have poisoned good Camillo's honor by making him kill a King. These are poor sins in comparison with your more monstrous sins.

"Another poor sin was your casting forth to crows your baby daughter, although a Devil would have shed tears in Hell before he had done such an action. Nor is it directly your fault that the young Prince, whose honorable thoughts — thoughts lofty for one so young — cleft the heart that could believe that a grossly foolish father had blemished his gracious dam. This is not, no, your responsibility, but this sin — lords, when I tell you what that sin is, mourn greatly — the Queen, the Queen, the sweetest, dearest creature is dead, and vengeance for her death has not yet dropped down from Heaven."

"May Heaven forbid it!" the first lord said.

"I say that the Queen is dead," Paulina said. "I will swear it. If you won't believe either my words or my oath, then go and see her for yourself. If you can bring color or luster to her lips and her eyes, make her body warm again, or make her breathe again, I'll serve you as I would the gods.

"But, oh, you tyrant! Do not repent these sins, for they are heavier than all your sorrow can expiate; therefore, do nothing except despair. A thousand knees kneeling for ten thousand years, the penitents naked and fasting upon a barren mountain during a perpetual winter storm could not move the gods to look in your direction and forgive your sins."

King Leontes said, "Go on. Continue. You can not criticize me too much; I have deserved for all tongues to talk their bitterest about me."

The first lord said to Paulina, "Say no more. Whatever happens as a result of the King's actions, you have committed a fault by being too bold in your speech to him."

"I am sorry," Paulina said. "All the faults I make, when I come to know that I have committed them, I repent. Look! I have showed too much the rashness of a woman: King Leontes is touched all the way to his noble heart."

She said to the King, "What's done and gone and what's past help should be past grief. Do not grieve because of my words. I beg you to instead punish me, who has reminded you of things that you should forget. Now, my good liege, sir, royal sir, forgive a foolish woman. The love I bore your Queen — ah, I am a fool again! — I'll speak of her no more, nor of your children. I will not remind you of my own husband, Antigonus, who is lost to me, too. Be patient and endure your suffering, and take your patience to you — I'll say nothing."

"You spoke well when you spoke the truth," King Leontes said. "You were speaking the absolute truth. I much prefer to hear you tell me my sins than to hear your words of pity. Please, take me to the dead bodies of my Queen and my son. They shall be buried in one grave. On the grave monument shall appear the causes of their death, which will always shame me.

"Once a day I'll visit the chapel where they lie, and I shall shed tears there as my recreation. As long as my health will allow me to do this exercise, so long I daily vow to do it.

"Come and lead me to these sorrows."

The word "recreation" meant "exercise," but repentance and suffering were to lead to re-creation. Repentance and suffering — and the grace of God — would make King Leontes a better person.

Antigonus, who was carrying Queen Hermione's infant daughter, and a mariner talked on the seacoast of Bohemia.

Bohemia is a landlocked country that has no seacoast. Strange things happen in Bohemia.

Antigonus asked, "You are certain then that our ship has reached a deserted part of Bohemia?"

"Yes, my lord," the mariner replied, "and I fear that we have landed at a bad time. The skies look grim and threaten immediate storms. By my conscience, I think that the Heavens are angry at us and frown at us because of this action you are about to do."

"May the sacred wills of the gods be done!" Antigonus said. "Go, get on board. Look after your ship. It will not be long before I return to it."

"Make your best speed, and do not go too far into the land. The weather is likely to be loud and foul; besides, this place is famous for the animals of prey that live here."

"Go now," Antigonus said. "I will follow you quickly."

The mariner replied, "I will be glad at heart when this business is over and done with."

He exited.

Antigonus said, "Come, poor babe. I have heard, but not believed, that the spirits of the dead may walk again. If such things are true, your mother appeared to me last night, for never was a dream so much like being awake. To me came a creature, sometimes her head leaning to one side and sometimes to the other. I never saw a vessel so filled with such sorrow and so beautiful. She was wearing pure white robes and looking like the true embodiment of saintliness. She approached the ship cabin where I lay; she bowed before me three times, and while she gasped for breath to begin some speech, her eyes became two spouts of tears. When her passionate outburst of sorrow was spent, she immediately said, 'Good Antigonus, since fate, against your better disposition, has made you the person to throw out my poor babe, according to your oath, let me tell you that Bohemia has very remote places. Take my daughter there, and then weep and leave it crying. And, because the babe is thought to be lost forever, call it Perdita, which means *the lost female*. Because of this ignoble business put on you by my husband, King Leontes, you shall never see your wife, Paulina, again.' And then, with shrieks, she melted into air.

"Although I was very frightened, I did eventually collect myself and thought this was real and not only sleep. Dreams are trifles. However, for this once, yes, superstitiously, I will be ruled by this vision. I believe that Queen Hermione has died."

He thought, *If what I saw is real, and I really did see the ghost of Queen Hermione, it must be the case that she is in Purgatory and so is repenting her sins. One of those sins must be adultery. Previously, I was sure that she was innocent of adultery, but now I believe that I was wrong.*

Antigonus was incorrect when he thought Queen Hermione had committed adultery; because of that, he felt that the god Apollo wanted the infant girl to be exposed to the elements. The gods often punish such mistakes.

He said, "I believe that Apollo wishes, since this baby is indeed the issue of King Polixenes, that it should here be laid, either to live or to die, upon the earth of its rightful father. You blossom, you infant girl, I hope that all may go well for you!

"Now I put you down here, and also I put down a document that states some of your history, and finally I put down a box containing gold and jewels. I hope that they, if fortune will allow it, will pay for your upbringing, pretty child, and I hope that something will remain that you will get when you come of age.

"The storm begins; poor wretch, because of your mother's sin you are exposed to what may follow your being thrown out! Weep I cannot, but my heart bleeds; and I am most accursed because I must do this because of the oath that I swore. Farewell! The day frowns more and more. You are likely to have too rough a lullaby. I never saw the sky to be so dim by day."

He heard the sounds of roaring and said, "A savage clamor! I hope that I can get aboard the ship!"

He saw a bear coming toward him and said, "This is the chase. I am being hunted. I am gone forever."

He ran away, pursued by the bear. Readers who someday see the bear on stage may think it is an actor in a bear costume.

An elderly shepherd arrived and said, "I wish there were no age between sixteen and twenty-three, or that youth would sleep during those years; for there is nothing between age sixteen and age twenty-three except getting wenches pregnant, upsetting old people, stealing, and fighting — here's an example! Would anyone but these boiled brains — hotheads — of nineteen to twenty-two years old hunt in this kind of weather? They have scared away two of my best sheep, which I fear the wolf will find sooner than I, their owner, will. If I find them anywhere, it will be by the seaside, grazing on ivy. God, send me good luck, if it be Thy will."

He saw the baby Perdita and said, "What have we here! May God have mercy on us. It is a baby, a very pretty baby! Is it a boy or a girl, I wonder? It is a pretty one — a very pretty one. Surely, it is the result of some escapade. Although I am not bookish, yet I can read that a waiting-gentlewoman is involved in this escapade. Some man has gone up the back stairs, or hidden in a trunk, or hidden behind a door. The man and woman who created this baby were warmer than the poor thing is here. I'll take it and raise it up out of pity for it, but I'll tarry until my son comes; he hallooed just a moment ago."

The old shepherd called, "Halloo!"

The old shepherd's son, who was nicknamed "Clown," called back, "Halloo!" He then walked to the old shepherd.

"What, are you so near? If you want to see a thing to talk about when you are dead and rotten, come here," the shepherd said.

Seeing that his son looked excited, he asked him, "What is wrong with you, man?"

Clown replied, "I have seen two such sights, by sea and by land! But I am not able to say it is a sea because it is now the sky. In this storm, the sky and the sea are so close that you cannot thrust the point of a pin between them."

"Tell me more," the shepherd said.

"I wish that you could see how the sea chafes, how it rages, how it swallows up the shore! But that's not the point. Oh, I heard the most piteous cries of the poor souls! Sometimes I could see them, and sometimes I could not see them. At one time the ship rose high and drilled the Moon with her mainmast, and then the ship sank low and was swallowed by foam and froth. The ship was stuck into the sea the way that you would stick a cork into a barrel.

"And then as for the man serving on land — I saw how the bear tore out his shoulder-bone; he cried to me for help and said his name was Antigonus and he was a nobleman. He was food served to the bear on land.

"But I also saw the end of the ship at sea. I saw the sea swallow it like a man would swallow a raisin that was floating in brandy that had been set on fire. But before the ship sank, the poor souls roared, and the sea mocked them; and I saw how the poor gentleman roared and the bear mocked him — both were roaring louder than the sea or weather."

"In the name of mercy, when did this happen, boy?"

"Just now. I have not even blinked since I saw these sights: the men are not yet cold under water, and the bear has not half dined on the gentleman. The bear is still eating him at this moment."

The shepherd said, "I wish that I had been near so I could have helped the old man!"

Clown, who did not believe that his father could have helped the old man, said, "I wish that you had been by the ship's side so you could have helped her. There your charity would have lacked footing."

Of course, no footing can be found at the top of the deep sea; in addition, a charity can lack proper footing — a foundation.

The shepherd said, "These are heavy matters, heavy matters! But look here, boy. Bless yourself now. You met with things dying, while I met with something newborn. Here's a sight for you. Look here, this is a rich shawl in which a squire's child would be carried to church so it can be baptized! Look here; here is a box. Pick it up, boy. Pick it up, and open it. So, let's see what it is. I remember that I was once told that the fairies would make me rich. I think that this child is a human child whom the fairies stole. What's inside the box, boy?"

Clown replied, "Old man, you are made. You are prosperous. As long as the sins of your youth are forgiven, you will live a good life. Gold is inside the box! Lots of gold!"

"This is fairy gold, boy," the shepherd said. "I am sure of it. Pick it up, and carry it, and let's go home by the quickest way. We are lucky, boy; and to always continue to be so requires nothing but secrecy. It is bad luck to tell people about the gifts of the fairies. Let my sheep go. Come, good boy, let's get home quickly."

"You go home quickly with these things you found," Clown said. "I'll go see if the bear has gone away from the gentleman and how much he has eaten.

Bears are never ill tempered except when they are hungry. If there is any of the gentleman left, I'll bury it."

"That's a good deed," the shepherd said. "If you can learn anything about the gentleman from what is left of him, come to me and take me to see him."

"Indeed, I will," Clown replied, "and you shall help me to put him in the ground."

"It is a lucky day for us, boy, and we'll do good deeds on it."

CHAPTER 4
— 4.1 —

The personification of Time, an old man who was winged and carried an hourglass, said, "I, one who pleases some, tests all, brings both joy and terror to both the good and the bad, and both makes and reveals errors, now take upon myself, in the name of Time, to use my wings and fly past time.

"Do not call me a criminal or my swift passage a crime now that I am sliding over sixteen years and leaving the events of that wide gap of time undescribed, since it is in my power to overthrow law. In one and the same hour (that I myself made) I can establish and obliterate traditions. Believe that I am the same now that I have always been; I was the same before the establishment of laws and customs as I am now with the current traditions that are now in vogue.

"I witnessed the times that started civilization and the times that started the most recent traditions now reigning, and I will see the glistening of this present time grow old, as my tale will now reveal to you.

"With your permission, I turn my hourglass and start a new hour. The events that you have been reading about are now sixteen years in the past. Other events have happened that you are unaware of, as you would be if you had been asleep.

"Let us leave behind King Leontes, who has been so sorrowful over the bad consequences of his foolish jealousy that he shuts himself up.

"Now imagine, gentle readers, that I am now in fair Bohemia. Remember well that I mentioned that King Polixenes has a son, and I now reveal to you his name: Florizel.

"Speeding on, let me tell you about Perdita, whose grace has grown as much as the admiration she receives has grown.

"What happens to her I prefer not to prophesy here; instead, let Time's news be known when it is brought forth, as it will be. A shepherd's daughter, and what happens to her, whom and which you now will read about, is the theme of Time.

"Whether or not you have spent your time worse than you are now doing, believe that Time himself says that he wishes earnestly you never will."

In the palace of King Polixenes in Bohemia, the King and Camillo were speaking.

"Please, good Camillo, ask me no more about this. It makes me ill to deny you anything, but if I were to grant you your request, it would be the death of me."

"It has been fifteen years since I last saw my country," Camillo said. "Although I have for the greater part of my life breathed air abroad, I desire to lay my bones there. I want Sicily to be the land I am buried in. Besides, the penitent King Leontes, my master, has sent for me. I may help alleviate his distressing sorrows, or so I flatter myself to think so, which is another spur to make me seek my departure from Bohemia."

"If you respect me, Camillo, do not wipe out the rest of your services to me by leaving me now. Your own goodness and competence have made me need you; it would have been better for me to have not had you serve me than to now be without you. You, having started some projects that no one else can sufficiently manage without your help, must either stay to execute them yourself or take away with you the very services you have done. If I have not enough rewarded you, as too much I cannot, I will take care to be more thankful to you, and my profit will be more service from you.

"Please speak no more about that fatal country, Sicily; the mere act of saying its name punishes me with the memory of that penitent, as you call him, and reconciled King Leontes, my brother, whose loss of his most precious Queen Hermione and children are even now to be freshly lamented."

He hesitated a moment and said, "Tell me, when did you last see Prince Florizel, my son? Kings are no less unhappy when their children do not act graciously than they are in losing their children when they have proven to have virtues."

Camillo replied, "Sir, it has been three days since I saw the Prince. What his business is that makes him happier than being here, I do not know, but I noted that he has been absent. He recently has spent much time away from court and spends less time doing his usual activities than he did formerly."

"I have noticed that, too, Camillo," Polixenes said, "and I have been and am worried about my son. I am worried enough that I have eyes under my service that are spying on him. From my spies I have received a report that he is seldom away from the house of a very humble shepherd, a man, they say, who from very poor circumstances, and beyond the knowledge and imagination of his neighbors, has acquired inestimable riches."

"I have heard of such a man, who has a daughter who is said to be very remarkable," Camillo said. "The reports of her are so widely spread that one would not think that she came from such a cottage."

"That's likewise part of what I learned from the reports I received," King Polixenes replied. "She is said to be remarkable, but I fear that she is the baited fishhook that plucks our son thither."

Concern about his son made him use the royal plural.

He continued, "You shall accompany us to the cottage, where we will, not appearing as what we are but instead wearing a disguise, have some conversation with the shepherd so we can ask him questions. Because of the shepherd's rusticity, I think it will not be difficult to get the reason for my son's going there.

"Please, be my partner now in this matter, and lay aside your thoughts of Sicily. Stay and help me; do not go to Sicily."

"I willingly obey your command."

"You are the best, Camillo! We must disguise ourselves."

— 4.3 —

Autolycus, a scamp who lacked morals, sang on a road near the shepherd's cottage. Autolycus was thoroughly selfish, but he was not below occasionally doing a good deed, as long as it happened by accident.

Autolycus sang, "*When daffodils begin to appear,*
"*With heigh! The doxy over the dale,*
"*Why, then comes in the sweet of the year;*
"*For the red blood reigns in the winter's pale.*
"*The white sheet bleaching on the hedge —*
"*With heigh, the sweet birds, oh, how they sing! —*
"*Does set my thievish tooth on edge;*
"*For a quart of ale is a dish fit for a King.*
"*The lark, that tirra-lyra chants,*
"*With heigh! With heigh! The thrush and the jay,*
"*Are summer songs for me and my aunts,*
"*While we lie tumbling in the hay.*"

Autolycus was singing about the arrival of spring, flowers, and songbirds. He was also singing about some of his major concerns in life: women and thievery. A doxy is a beggar woman, who is also often the girlfriend of a beggar. By "aunts," Autolycus meant "prostitutes." Because it was spring, housewives were doing laundry and leaving their sheets outside to dry. As a thief, Autolycus was on the lookout for sheets so he could steal them, sell them, and buy ale.

Autolycus said, "I have served Prince Florizel, and in my time I have worn the very best velvet clothing, but now I am out of service — I have no position."

He sang, "*But shall I go mourn for that, my dear?*
"*The pale Moon shines by night:*
"*And when I wander here and there,*
"*I then do most go right.*
"*If tinkers may have leave to live,*
"*And bear the sow-skin budget,*
"*Then my account I well may give,*
"*And in the stocks avouch it.*"

As a wandering thief, Autolycus believed that all roads led the right way. It did not matter to him where he went. But he was concerned about being punished for being a vagabond and a thief, one punishment for which was being put in the stocks. The stocks immobilized the thief's hands and/or feet, and if someone in the crowd, such as one of the thief's victims, wanted, he or she could torment the thief. Autolycus, however, planned to claim that he was a wandering tinker. He would carry a pigskin budget, aka bag, of the kind that tinkers used to carry their tools. Of course, Autolycus hoped to keep his bag filled with stolen loot.

Autolycus said, "My trade is sheets; I steal them and sell them. When the kite builds a nest in the spring, housewives need to look after their lesser linen because these birds will steal small pieces of linen and use them to line their nests. My father named me Autolycus. Being, as I am, littered when the planet Mercury was ascendant, according to the astrologers, my father was likewise a snapper-up of trifles that housewives did not carefully enough watch."

Autolycus knew that he had a good name for the kind of person he was. The pagan god Mercury was the patron god of thieves, and with a mortal woman named Chinoe, he had fathered a child named Autolycus, who like his father, Mercury, was a skilled thief.

Autolycus continued, "With die and drab I purchased this caparison. In other words, with gambling and whores, I 'purchased' this outfit of rags that I am wearing. My main source of revenue is the silly cheat, aka petty thievery. Gallows and hard knocks are too powerful on the highway: Being beaten and/ or hanged is a terror to me, and I hope to escape being punished for petty thievery — let the officers of the law pursue those who commit grand thievery! As for the life to come, I sleep and do not think about it."

Seeing Clown, the old shepherd's son, walking toward him, Autolycus said to himself, "A prize! A prize!"

A pirate seeing a ship that he could rob would also say, "A prize! A prize!"

Clown was trying to figure out how much money his father would make during the forthcoming sheep shearing: "Let me see. Every eleven sheep yield a tod of wool: about 28 pounds. Every tod yields one pound and odd shillings; fifteen hundred sheep will be shorn. What total will the sale of the wool come to?"

Autolycus said to himself, "If the trap works, the woodcock's mine."

A woodcock is a proverbially stupid bird that is easily caught in a trap.

Clown said, "I cannot do it without counting-disks. Let me see. What am I to buy for our sheep-shearing feast? Let me read my list. Three pounds of sugar, five pounds of currants, rice — what will this sister of mine, Perdita, do with rice? But my father has made her mistress of the feast, and she makes the most of it. She has made twenty-four nosegays for the shearers. All of them sing parts in songs that are written for three men, and they are very good singers, but most of them are tenors and basses and cannot sing treble. Only one Puritan is among them, and he sings psalms to the gay music of hornpipes. I must have saffron to color the pear pies, and mace, which is a spice. How many dates? None, dates are not on my list. Seven nutmegs; a root or two of ginger, but that I may ask for as a favor; four pounds of prunes, and as many pounds of sun-ripened raisins."

Autolycus set his trap. He lay on the ground and acted as if he had been beaten and was in pain.

He cried, "I am sorry that I was ever born!"

Clown said, "In the name of me —"

He may have been about to say, "In the name of mercy."

"Oh, help me, help me!" Autolycus said. "Pluck these rags off my body and then let me die, die!"

"Alas, poor soul!" Clown said. "You need more rags to put on you, rather than have these rags taken off."

"Sir, the loathsomeness of these rags offends me more than the stripes I have received from being beaten; the stripes are mighty ones and in the millions."

"Alas, poor man!" Clown said. "A million stripes from being beaten is rather a lot of stripes."

"I have been robbed, sir, and beaten; my money and apparel have been taken from me, and these detestable rags were put upon me."

"Who did it?" Clown asked. "A robber on horseback, or on foot?"

"He was on foot, sweet sir; he was a footman."

"I can believe that," Clown said, "because of the garments he has left with you. Anyone who can afford a horse can afford better clothing than this. If this is a horseman's coat you are wearing, it has seen very hot service in battle. Give me your hand. I'll help you up. Come, give me your hand."

"Good sir, gently help me up," Autolycus said. "I am in pain."

"Alas, poor soul!"

"Oh, good sir, gently, good sir! I fear, sir, my shoulder blade has been dislocated."

"How are you?" Clown asked. "Can you stand now?"

Autolycus said while picking Clown's pocket, "Gently, dear sir; good sir, gently. You have done me a charitable deed."

Clown asked, "Do you need any money? I have a little money that I can give you."

Autolycus, who did not want Clown to reach for his money and find that it was missing, replied, "No, good sweet sir; no, but thank you, sir. I have a kinsman not more than three quarters of a mile from here, to whom I was going. I shall there have money, or anything I want. Don't give me any money, please; that would kill my heart."

"What kind of fellow was he who robbed you?"

"He was a fellow, sir, whom I have known to go about with troll-my-dames, a game that women often play and gamble on. I know that he was once a servant of Prince Florizel. I cannot tell, good sir, for which of his virtues it was, but he was certainly whipped out of the court."

Clown said, "His vices, you should say; no virtues are whipped out of the court. People at court cherish virtues and want them to stay, and yet virtues stay only a short time before leaving."

"In the case of this man, 'vices' is the right word, I would say, sir," Autolycus said, "I know this man well. He has been in the past a traveling showman with a monkey, and then he was a process-server, aka a bailiff, and then he traveled with a puppet show that told the story of the Prodigal Son, and then he married a tinker's wife within a mile of where my land and living lie. Finally, having tried his hand at many knavish professions, he settled on being only a rogue. Some call him Autolycus."

"Damn him!" Clown said. "He is a thief, I declare by my life — he is a thief! He haunts rural festivals, fairs, and bear baitings; those are the places he commits his crimes."

"That is very true, sir," Autolycus said. "He is the rogue who put me in these rags."

"There is not a more cowardly rogue in all Bohemia," Clown said. "If you had only looked mean and spit at him, he would have run."

"I must confess to you, sir, that I am no fighter," Autolycus said. "I am false of heart that way, and I bet that he knew it."

"How are you now?"

"Sweet sir, much better than I was; I can stand and walk. I will now take my leave of you, and walk slowly towards my kinsman's."

"Do you want me to walk with you there?" Clown asked.

"No, good-faced sir; no, sweet sir."

"Then may you fare well," Clown said. "I must go buy spices for our sheep-shearing feast."

"May God make you prosper, sweet sir!"

Clown departed.

Autolycus said to himself, "Your purse is not hot enough for you to purchase your spices. Money is not burning a hole in your pocket because now you have no money. I'll be with you at your sheep shearing, too. If I cannot make this trick lead me to another, and if the shearers do not prove to be my sheep, let my name be taken out of the roll of thieves and put in the book of virtue!"

He sang, "*Jog on, jog on, the footpath way,*

"*And merrily jump the stile-a:*

"*A merry heart goes all the day,*

"*A sad heart tires in a mile-a.*"

Prince Florizel and Perdita talked together in front of the old shepherd's cottage. Both were dressed for the festival. Florizel was dressed as a shepherd because he was in disguise, but because Perdita was the Hostess of the Festival, she was dressed in fine clothing, and she was carrying flowers.

Florizel said, "Your fine clothing, which you do not normally wear, gives you a new life. You seem to be a different person. No longer are you a shepherdess; instead, you are Flora, goddess of spring, as she looks during the beginning of April. This sheep-shearing festival is like a meeting of the minor gods, and it is as if you are the Queen of the Festival."

"Sir, my gracious lord, it does not become me to protest your exaggerations," Perdita replied. "Pardon me for even mentioning them! Your social position is high, and everyone in the country knows who you are, but you have disguised yourself by wearing the clothing of a shepherd. I am a lowly maiden, but now I am wearing the fancy clothing of a goddess. Except that every feast has its share of foolishness and the feeders digest the foolishness because they are accustomed to seeing it at feasts, I would blush to see you in such clothing, and I believe that I would faint if I saw my reflection in a mirror."

"I bless the time when my good falcon made her flight across your father's grounds," Florizel said. "That is how I came to meet you."

"May Jupiter give you a good reason to be happy about meeting me!" Perdita said. "As for myself, the great difference in our social status causes me to feel dread; you, because of your high social status, are not accustomed to fear anything. Even now I tremble to think that your father, by some accident, should pass this way as you did. Oh, may the Fates give you, dressed as you are in shepherd's clothing, good fortune! How would your father look if he were to see his so noble work so vilely bound? You are like a good book that has been badly bound. What would your father say? How would I, dressed in all this unaccustomed finery, stand the sternness of his presence?"

"Foresee nothing but jollity and happiness," Florizel said. "The gods themselves, humbling their deities because of love, have even taken the shapes of beasts upon themselves. Jupiter, the King of the gods, became a bull and bellowed so that he could be with the mortal woman Europa. The green

Neptune, god of the sea, became a ram and bleated so that he could be with the mortal woman Theophane. The fire-robed god, Golden Apollo, the god of the Sun, became a poor humble shepherd, like me, so that he could be with the mortal woman Issa, as we learn from Ovid's *Metamorphoses*.

"Their transformations were never for a masterpiece of beauty such as yours, and their lusts were never as chaste as mine, since my desires do not overwhelm my honor, nor do my lusts burn hotter than my faith. My love for you is honorable."

"But, sir, your resolution cannot hold when it is opposed, as it must be, by the power of King Polixenes, your father. One of these two things must happen, and we will find out which one at that time: either you must change your purpose, or I must change my life."

If Florizel changed his purpose, he would obey his father and not marry Perdita. If Florizel did not change his purpose, then Perdita would change her life. One way for her to change her life would be to run away with Florizel, but Perdita may have meant that the King would force her to change her life by giving up Florizel.

"Dearest Perdita," Florizel said, "do not darken the mirth of the feast with these unlikely and negative thoughts. Either I'll be yours, my fair one; or if I cannot, then I will not be my father's son. I shall not be any good to myself or to anyone if I cannot be yours. To this I am and will be most constant — it does not matter if destiny and fate oppose me.

"Be merry, gentle one. Strangle such thoughts as these with the sights of the feast that is starting. Your guests are coming, so brighten your countenance and smile as if today were the day of celebration of that nuptial that we two have sworn shall come. I swear that we shall be wed."

"May Lady Fortune bring us good luck!" Perdita said.

Florizel said, "Look, your guests are approaching. Devote yourself to entertaining them sprightly, and let's be red-faced with mirth."

The old shepherd, Clown, and other revelers walked toward them, including the shepherdesses Mopsa and Dorcas. Disguised with false beards, King Polixenes and Camillo also walked toward them.

The old shepherd said, "Come on, daughter! When my old wife was alive, on this feast day she served as keeper of the pantry, keeper of the wine cellar, cook, head of the household, and servant of the household. She welcomed all and served all. She would sing her song and dance her turn. Now she would be here, at the upper end of the table, and then she would be in the middle. She would lean over the shoulder of one man and then of another. Her face would be on fire because of her labor, and the drink she took to quench the fire she would use to toast each guest. You are shy and retiring as if you were a guest and not the Hostess of the Feast. Please, greet warmly these two friends whom we do not know; that is the way to make good friends. By knowing them, we become better friends. Come, quench your blushes and present yourself as the person whom you are: the Hostess of the Feast."

The disguised King Polixenes said, "Do so, and bid us welcome to your sheep-shearing. If you do that, your good flock shall prosper."

Perdita said to him, "Sir, welcome. My father wishes me to serve as the hostess on this day."

To the disguised Camillo, she said, "You're welcome, sir."

She then said, "Give me those flowers there, Dorcas."

Dorcas handed her the flowers, and Perdita gave them to the two disguised old men, saying, "Reverend sirs, for you there's the flower rosemary for remembrance and the flower rue for grace; these keep their appearance and scent all the winter long. May both of you have grace and remembrance, and welcome to our shearing!"

The disguised King Polixenes said, "Shepherdess, you are a pretty girl — you do well to give us flowers that suit our age."

"Sir, the year is growing older, although it is not yet the death of the summer or the birth of trembling winter. Therefore, the fairest flowers of the season are carnations and streaked, multicolored gillyflowers, which some call nature's bastards. We do not have that kind of flower in our garden, and I do not care to get cuttings of them to put in our garden."

The disguised King Polixenes asked, "Why, gentle maiden, do you neglect them and do not want them in your garden?"

"I have heard it said that the streaks of color in these flowers were created by gardeners and not by Nature," Perdita replied.

The disguised King Polixenes said, "Let us say that is true. Should it matter? How is Nature made better? Nature is made better by no means except what Nature makes. If a gardener is able to breed flowers that have beautiful streaks of color, so what? Nature made the gardener. A man may add art to Nature, but Nature made the art that made the man.

"You see, sweet maiden, we marry a gentler scion to the wildest stock, and make a bark of baser kind conceive by a bud of nobler race. For example, we can graft a branch of a tree that bears tasty apples to a crabapple tree. This improves Nature — rather, it changes Nature — but the art that creates the change is itself created by Nature. The gardener must work in accordance with what Nature teaches him."

"That is so," Perdita said.

"Then make your garden rich in gillyflowers, and do not call them bastards."

Perdita had another reason for not wanting to have gillyflowers in the garden. The colors in gillyflowers reminded many people of painting, which was associated with the makeup worn by prostitutes. Also, she regarded makeup as unnatural.

She said to the disguised King Polixenes, "I'll not put a spade in earth to create a hole to plant one cutting of them, no more than were I painted I would wish this youth to say it were well and only because of the makeup would he desire to make me pregnant."

She said to the disguised Camillo, "Here's flowers for you. Hot lavender, mints, savory, marjoram. Here is the marigold, which goes to bed with the Sun and with him rises, weeping tears of dew. It closes its petals when the Sun sets and opens them when the Sun rises. These are flowers of middle summer, and I think they are given to men of middle age. You're very welcome here."

The disguised Camillo complimented her beauty: "I would stop grazing, if I were one of your flock, and live only by gazing."

"If you were to do that," Perdita replied, "you would become so lean that the windy blasts of January would blow right through you."

She said to Florizel, "Now, my fairest friend, I wish that I had some flowers of the spring that might become your time of day —"

She then said to the young shepherdesses, Mopsa and Dorcas, "— and yours, and yours, who still wear upon your virgin branches your growing maidenhood: You wear the garments of young virgins."

Perdita then said, "Proserpina, I wish I had the spring flowers that you dropped when Dis, god of the underworld, frightened you by kidnapping you to make you his wife. From his chariot, you dropped daffodils, which come up in the spring before the swallow dares to return from the South and which charm the winds of March with beauty. You dropped violets that droop, but are sweeter than the eyelids of the goddess Juno or the breath of the goddess Venus. You dropped pale primroses that die unmarried, before they can behold the bright Sun in his strength. They die unmarried — because they grow in the shade and are unkissed by the Sun — in the early spring before the Sun reaches its full strength in the summer; this is a malady that often affects maidens."

The disease called green sickness, which is known today as hypochromic anemia, sometimes afflicted young girls in this society. The disease gave the sufferer's skin a greenish tint.

Perdita continued, "Proserpina also dropped bold oxlips and the crown imperial, and lilies of all kinds, the flower-de-luce being one! I lack these flowers, or I would make garlands of them for you, Mopsa and Dorcas, and I would make my sweet friend, Florizel, garlands that I would strew all over him!"

"What, like a corpse?" Florizel said.

In this society, people strewed flowers over corpses.

"No, like a riverbank for lovers to lie and play on," Perdita said, "Not like a corpse; or if like a body, a body not to be buried, but one that is alive and in my arms.

"Come, take your flowers. I think that I am playing the Queen as I have seen people do in Whitsuntide festivals. Surely, this fancy robe I am wearing has changed my disposition and personality."

"Whatever you do betters whatever you have already done," Florizel said. "When you speak, sweetheart, I want you to speak forever. When you sing, I want you to sing while you are buying and selling, while you are giving alms, while you are praying, and while you are doing other things. When you dance, I wish that you were a wave of the sea, so that you might forever do nothing but continually move — always and forever. Each thing you do, unique in each detail, crowns whatever you are doing at whatever time, and all your actions are supreme."

Perdita said to Florizel, who was using a pseudonym, "Oh, Doricles, your praises of me are excessive. Except that your youth, and the true blood that peeps fairly through your skin, plainly show that you are an unstained shepherd, I might fear, if I were wise, my Doricles, that you wooed me the false way."

Perdita knew that Florizel's intentions toward her were honest; otherwise, she might have been afraid that he was trying to flatter her into bed. In fact, Florizel was unstained. True, he was not a shepherd, but Perdita had to call him that because they were in the presence of other people.

Florizel replied, "I think you have as little reason to fear me as I have intentions to do anything that would make you fear me. But come; let us dance, please. Give me your hand, my Perdita. In this way, turtledoves form a pair. They mate for life and never mean to part."

"I swear that is true," Perdita said.

Florizel and Perdita danced.

The disguised King Polixenes said, "This is the prettiest low-born lass that ever ran on the grassy ground. Everything she does or seems to be makes her appear to be better than a peasant. She seems as if she is too noble for this place. It seems that she ought to be a Princess, not a shepherdess."

"Doricles is telling her something that makes her blush," Camillo said. "Truly, she is the Queen of curds and cream — she is the May Queen."

Clown said to the band of musicians, "Come on, strike up the band! Start playing!"

He wanted to dance with Mopsa, so a jealous Dorcas said, "Mopsa is your partner in the dance, which involves kissing. Give her some garlic to eat so it will improve her breath and her kissing."

An indignant Mopsa said, "Hey!"

Clown said, "No arguing. No arguing. We need to be on our best manners here."

Clown and Mopsa joined a dance of shepherds and shepherdesses.

The disguised King Polixenes asked, "Please, good shepherd, tell me who this handsome shepherd is who is dancing with your daughter?"

"They call him Doricles," the old shepherd said, "and he boasts that he has lots of good pastureland, but he has told me this himself, and I believe it — he looks honest. He says he loves my daughter; I think so, too. Never has the Moon gazed upon the water the way he so often stands and looks into my daughter's eyes as if he were reading them. To speak plainly, I think there is not half a kiss' difference in the love one feels for the other — they love each other a lot, and equally."

The disguised King Polixenes said, "She dances well."

"That is how she does everything," the old shepherd said, "although I should be silent since I am biased. But if young Doricles marries her, she shall bring him good things that he does not dream of."

A servant entered and said to the old shepherd, "Master, if you could hear the peddler who is at the door, you would never dance again to a drum and fife; no, the bagpipe could not move you. This peddler sings several different tunes faster than you can count money; he utters them as if he had eaten and lived on ballads and all men's ears were glued to his tunes."

Clown said, "He could never have come at a better time; he shall come in. I love a ballad only too well, if it has sad lyrics set to a merry tune, or if it is a very pleasant thing indeed and sung sadly and lamentably."

The servant said, "He has songs for man or woman, of all sizes."

The servant meant that the songs were of various lengths.

The servant continued, "No haberdasher can so fit his customers with gloves as the peddler can fit his customers with ballads. He has the prettiest love-songs for maidens; the love-songs are without bawdry, which is strange and unusual. They have such delicate refrains of dildos and fadings, '*jump her and thump her,*' and where some dirty-mouthed rascal would, as it were, mean mischief and break a foul gap into the song so he can make a dirty joke, the peddler makes the maiden say, '*Whoop, do me no harm, good man.*' The maiden puts the dirty-minded man off and slights him with '*Whoop, do me no harm, good man.*'"

The servant apparently did not know the meaning of "dildo" when he said that the peddler did not sing bawdy songs. The servant also apparently did not know that many of the other words the peddler said and many of the lyrics the peddler sang were bawdy in nature.

The disguised King Polixenes said about the peddler, "This is a splendid fellow."

"Believe me," Clown said, "you are talking about an wonderfully inventive fellow."

He then asked the servant, "Has he any wares that are not shop-soiled?"

The servant replied, "He has ribbons of all the colors in the rainbow. He has points more than all the lawyers in Bohemia can learnedly handle, although they come to him by the gross."

The points were laces that were used to attach hose to a jacket, but the servant was also punning on legal points.

The servant continued, "He has linen tapes, caddis-ribbons for garters, and delicate fabrics such as cambrics and lawns for dressmaking. Why, he sings a song about the stuff he has for sale. He sings about and praises his wares as if they were gods or goddesses; you would think a smock were a she-angel, he sings such praise about the sleeve cuffs and the embroidery on the front of it."

"Please bring him in," Clown said, "and let him approach while singing."

Perdita said, "Warn him not to use any scurrilous words in his tunes."

The servant left to tell the peddler to come in.

"Some of these peddlers," Clown said, "have more in them than you would think, sister."

"Yes, good brother," Perdita said, "or more than I wish to think."

Autolycus, who was disguised enough that Clown did not recognize him, entered the scene. (He was wearing a false beard.) He had put the money that he had stolen from Clown to good use. He sang this song about the wares he had for sale:

"Lawn as white as driven snow;

"Crape black as ever was a crow;

"Gloves as perfumed as damask roses;

"Masks for faces and for noses;

"Black bead bracelet, necklace amber,

"Perfume for a lady's chamber;

"Golden coifs and stomachers,

"For my lads to give their dears.

"Pins and poking-sticks of steel,

"What maidens need from head to heel.

"Come buy from me, come; come and buy, come and buy;

"Buy, lads, or else your lasses will cry. Come and buy."

Lawn is a kind of linen. Stomachers are stiff embroidered bodices, and poking-sticks are used to maintain ruffs.

Clown said to the peddler, Autolycus, "If I were not in love with Mopsa, you would get no money from me; but being as enthralled and in bondage to love as I am, it will lead to the bondage of certain ribbons and gloves. You will tie them into a bundle after I buy them."

The archaic meaning of "enthrall" is "to enslave." A "thrall" is a slave.

"I was promised the ribbons and gloves as gifts in time for the feast, but they are not too late now," Mopsa said.

"He has promised you more than that, or there are liars," Dorcas said.

"He has paid you all he promised you," Mopsa said. "Maybe he has given you more than he promised, and it will shame you to give to him that extra back again."

Dorcas and Mopsa were fighting over Clown. Dorcas had been Clown's girlfriend, but Mopsa was now his girlfriend. Mopsa may have been hinting that the extra that Clown had given Dorcas was a child and that Dorcas would give Clown the child after it was born.

Clown, who was embarrassed by the fighting, complained, "Are there no manners left among maidens? Will they wear their undergarments where they should bear their faces?"

He felt that they were airing dirty laundry in public, and he felt that this conversation, if made at all, ought to be made in private.

He continued, "Is there not milking-time, or when you are going to bed, or when you are in front of the kiln-hole, to whistle off these secrets? Can't you talk about this at those more private times? Do you have to be tittle-tattling in front of all our guests? It is good that our guests are whispering so that we cannot hear what they are saying. Clam up your tongues, and say not a word more. Tie up your tongue as one could tie up the clapper of a bell."

"I have said what I had to say," Mopsa said. "Come, you promised to give me a tawdry-lace and a pair of sweet gloves."

In this society, gloves were perfumed, and a tawdry-lace was a brightly colored scarf that was worn around the neck.

"Haven't I told you how I was cheated on the road and lost all my money?" Clown said to Mopsa.

Autolycus said, "Indeed, sir, conmen are abroad; therefore, men ought to be wary."

"Fear not, man," Clown said. "You shall lose nothing here."

"I hope that you are right, sir," Autolycus said, "because I have about me many parcels of value."

"What do you have here?" Clown asked. "Ballads?"

"Please, buy some," Mopsa said. "I dearly love a ballad in print because then we are sure they are true."

"Here's one set to a very sad tune," Autolycus said. "It is about how a usurer's wife was brought to bed of twenty moneybags at a burden and how she longed to eat adders' heads and sliced, broiled toads."

One way to interpret what Autolycas had said was that a usurer's wife had given birth to twenty moneybags all at once. Another way to interpret it was that a usurer's wife had been persuaded by the gift of twenty moneybags to go to bed with the giver — her husband? — and bear the burden of his weight on her.

"Is it true, do you think?" Mopsa asked.

"Very true, and only a month old," Autolycus replied.

"May God keep me from marrying a usurer!" Dorcas said.

"Here's the midwife's name on it as a witness," Autolycas said. "Her name is Mistress Taleporter, and here are the names of five or six honest wives who were present. Why should I carry lies abroad?"

"Please," Mopsa said to Clown, "buy it."

"Come on, set it aside," Clown said, "and let's first see more ballads; we'll buy the other things soon."

Autolycus said, "Here's another ballad. This one is about a fish that appeared upon the coast on Wednesday on the eightieth of April, forty thousand fathoms above water, and sang this ballad against the hard hearts of maidens. People think that the fish was a woman who was turned into a cold fish because she would not exchange flesh — have sex — with one who loved her. The ballad is as sad as it is true. The ballad is pitiful."

"Is it true, too, do you think?" Dorcas asked.

"Five justices have certified that it is true, and there were more witnesses than my pack will hold," Autolycus replied.

"Lay it aside, too," Clown said. "Let's see another."

"This is a merry ballad, but it is a very pretty one," Autolycas said.

"Let's have some merry ones," Mopsa said.

"Why, this is a very merry one and goes to the tune of 'Two maids wooing a man.' There's scarcely a maiden westward who is not singing it," Autolycas said. "This song is in demand, I can tell you."

"We can both sing it," Mopsa said to Dorcas.

She then said to Autolycus, "If you'll take a part —" then she said to Clown, "— you shall hear it; it is in three parts."

"We learned the tune a month ago," Dorcas said.

"I can bear my part," Autolycas said. "You must know that singing is my occupation. Let's start."

Autolycus sang, "*Get you hence, for I must go*

"*Where it does not suit you to know.*"

Dorcas sang, "*Whither?*"

Mopsa sang, "*Oh, whither?*"

Dorcas sang, "*Whither?*"

Mopsa sang, "*It becomes your oath full well,*

"*You to me your secrets tell.*"

Dorcas sang, "*Me, too — let me go thither.*"

Mopsa sang, "*Or you go to the farm or mill.*"

Dorcas sang, "*If to either, you do evil.*"

Autolycus sang, "*Neither.*"

Dorcas sang, "*What, neither?*"

Autolycus sang, "*Neither.*"

Dorcas sang, "*You have sworn to be my love.*"

Mopsa sang, "*You have sworn it more to me.*

"*Then whither do you go? Tell us, whither?*"

Clown said to Mopsa and Dorcas, "We'll sing this song ourselves soon. My father and the gentlemen are having a serious talk, and we'll not trouble them."

He said to Autolycus, "Come, carry your pack and follow me. Girls, I'll buy for you both. Peddler, we want to have the first choice. Follow me, girls."

Clown exited with Mopsa and Dorcas.

Autolycus said, "And you shall pay well for them."

He followed them, singing this song:

"*Will you buy any tape,*

"*Or lace for your cape,*

"*My dainty duck, my dear-a?*

"Any silk, any thread,

"Any trifles for your head,

"Of the newest and finest, finest wear-a?

"Come to the peddler;

"Money's a meddler

"That does offer for sale all men's ware-a."

The last two lines meant, "Money gets involved in everything, and it keeps everything in circulation."

A servant said to the old shepherd, "Master, there are three drivers of carts, three shepherds, three cowherds, and three swineherds, who have made themselves all men of hair by wearing animal skins. They call themselves Saltiers, or Leaping Satyrs, and they have a dance that the wenches say is a gallimaufry, aka hodgepodge, of gambols, because they — the wenches — are not in it, but the Saltiers themselves are of the opinion that if it is not too rough for some who know little but the genteel game of bowling, it will plentifully please the audience."

"Away with them!" the old shepherd said. "We'll have none of it. We have had too much low-down tomfoolery already."

He said to the disguised King Polixenes, "I know, sir, that we weary you."

The disguised King Polixenes replied, "You weary those who refresh and entertain us. Please, let us see these four trios of country workers."

"One trio of them, by their own report, sir, has danced before the King; and even the worst of the trios jumps twelve foot and a half by the furniture maker's ruler," the servant said.

"Stop your prating," the old shepherd said. "Since these good men would like to see their dance, let them come in, but quickly."

"Why, they are waiting at the door, sir," the servant said, and then he left to carry out his orders.

The twelve Satyrs danced — wildly — and the old shepherd and the disguised King Polixenes talked.

After the dance, the disguised King Polixenes said to the old shepherd, "Father, you'll learn more about that soon."

In their society, old men were often addressed as "father" as a term of respect. It did not necessarily mean that the old man was the biological father of the person addressing him.

The disguised King Polixenes went to Camillo and asked, "Has the obvious love relationship of my son the Prince and this young shepherdess gone too far? Yes. It is time to part them. The old shepherd is a simple man and has told me what I need to know."

The disguised King Polixenes said to Florizel, his son the Prince, "How now, fair shepherd! Your heart is full of something that takes your mind away from feasting. Truly, when I was young and in love as you are now, I was wont to load my girlfriend with small gifts. I would have ransacked the peddler's silken treasury and have poured it upon her to gain her approval; you, however, have let the peddler leave and have bought nothing from him. If your lass should misinterpret this as you lacking love or generosity, you would be at a loss for a reply, at least if you want to make her happy."

Florizel replied, "Old sir, I know that she does not prize such trifles as those that the peddler has. The gifts she looks for from me are packed and locked up in my heart, which I have given to her already, but not delivered. I love her, but I am not yet legally married to her."

He said to Perdita, "Listen as I utter vows that I shall keep all my life. I will say them with this ancient sir as my witness; he, it seems, has once loved! I take your hand, this hand, as soft as the down of a dove and as white as it or the tooth of a dark-skinned Ethiopian, or the fanned snow that's sifted by the northern blasts of icy wind twice over."

"What can follow such an elaborate preface?" the disguised King Polixenes asked. "How prettily the young shepherd seems to wash and make whiter the hand that was already white!"

He said to Florizel, "I have interrupted you. Continue your speech; let me hear what you have to say."

"Do, and be a witness to it," Florizel said.

"And shall this my neighbor be a witness, too?" the disguised King Polixenes asked, indicating the disguised Camillo.

"And he shall be a witness, and more than he. Let men, the Earth, the Heavens, and all know that, if I were crowned the most imperial monarch, and if I were very worthy of the crown, and if I were the handsomest youth who ever made eyes swerve to look at him, and if I had strength and knowledge more than was ever mortal man's, I would not prize them without her love. For her

I would employ them all. I would commend them to the service of Perdita or condemn them to their own perdition. I want to marry Perdita."

"Well spoken," the disguised King Polixenes said.

"This shows a sound affection," the disguised Camillo said.

"But, my daughter," the old shepherd asked, "do you feel the same way about him?"

"I cannot speak as well as he, not even close," Perdita replied, "but all meaning will be the same. I understand that he feels about me the same way I feel about him."

Using a dressmaking metaphor, she said, "By the pattern of my own thoughts, I cut out the purity of his." In other words, she was saying that the purity of her thoughts validated the purity of his thoughts because her thoughts mirrored his. She added, "I want to marry him."

The old shepherd rejoiced and said, "Hold hands! You have made a bargain!"

The old shepherd said to the disguised King Polixenes and the disguised Camillo, "Unknown friends, you shall bear witness to this engagement. I give my daughter to him, and I will make her portion equal his. My daughter's dowry will equal what he brings to the marriage."

"Oh, her equal portion must be the virtue of your daughter," Florizel said. "Once a certain person is dead, I shall possess more than you can dream of now; later you can marvel at all I possess. But, come on, let us make a legal and binding engagement before these witnesses."

The old shepherd said to Florizel, "Come, hold out your hand," and he said to Perdita, "Daughter, hold out your hand."

"Wait," the disguised King Polixenes said to Florizel. "Wait a moment, young shepherd, please. Do you have a father?"

"Yes, I do, but what about him?"

"Does he know about this?"

"He does not, and he shall not."

The disguised King Polixenes said, "In my opinion a father is very suitable to be a guest at the wedding of his son. Please tell me these things. Has your father grown incapable of reason? Has he become stupid with age and mind-altering illnesses? Can he speak? Can he hear? Can he distinguish one man from another man? Can he manage his own estate? Is he bed-ridden? Is he in his second childhood?"

"No, good sir," Florizel replied. "He has his health, and he is stronger than most men his age."

"By my white beard," the disguised King Polixenes said, "You are doing him, if what you said is true, a wrong that is somewhat unfilial. A good son would not treat his father this way. It is reasonable that my son should choose a wife for himself, but it is also reasonable that the father, all of whose joy comes from fair and good and worthy descendants, should give his advice when it comes to making such a choice."

"I agree with what you say, my grave sir," Florizel said, "but for some other reasons, which are not suitable for you to know, I will not tell my father about this engagement."

"Let him know it," the disguised King Polixenes said.

"He shall not."

"Please, let him know it."

"No, he must not."

The old shepherd said to Florizel, "Let him know, my son. When he knows your choice, he will have no reason to grieve. Perdita will be an excellent wife for you."

"Come, come, he must not," Florizel said. "Let us make a legal and binding engagement."

Pulling off his fake beard, King Polixenes said, "I now make for you a binding divorce, young sir. I dare not call you my son. You are too base to be acknowledged as my son. You, a scepter's heir, are in love with a shepherd's crook — a shepherdess!"

He said to the old shepherd, "You old traitor, I am sorry that by hanging you I can shorten your life by only one week."

He said to Perdita, "And you, young masterpiece of excellent witchcraft, you cunning young witch, who of course must know the Prince, that royal fool you are involved with —"

Shocked at seeing his King, and shocked at knowing that his King was angry at him and his daughter, the old shepherd said, "Oh, my heart!"

King Polixenes said to Perdita, "I'll have your beauty scratched with briers, and you will be made more homely and lowly than your social status."

He said to his son, Prince Florizel, "As for you, fond and foolish boy, if I should ever know that you even sigh because you shall never again see this trifle of a woman — and I do mean never — we will bar you from succession. You will never become King. We will not regard you as being of our blood — no, you will not be our kin. You will be a more distant relative to me than is Deucalion, the only man to survive the Great Flood and therefore the father of all men. Listen to us. Follow us back to the court."

Continuing to use the royal plural, he said to the old shepherd, "You churl, for this time, although we are full of displeasure at you, yet we free you from the deadly blow of it. We will not kill you at this time."

He said to Perdita, "And as for you, enchantment, you are beautiful, and full of virtue, although you are low born. You are worthy enough to marry a herdsman. Yes, you are also worthy enough to marry my son — if he were not a Prince. Because of his actions, however, my son has made himself unworthy of you. If ever henceforth you leave these rural latches open so that my son can enter here, or if you ever use your arms to make a hoop around his body with your embraces, I will devise a death as cruel for you as you are vulnerable to it."

He departed.

Perdita said, "Despite the King's threat to have me killed, I was not much afraid because once or twice I was about to speak and tell him plainly that the same Sun that shines upon his court does not hide its visage from our cottage but looks on all alike."

She said to Florizel, "Will it please you, sir, to leave? I told you what would come of this. Please, take care of yourself and do not endanger your position — make sure that you will someday become King. Being engaged to you has been a dream of mine — but now that I am awake, I'll Queen it not an inch farther. Instead, I will milk my ewes and weep."

Camillo, still disguised, said to the old shepherd, "How are you, father? Speak before you die. Keeping your emotions bottled up can kill you."

"I cannot speak," the old shepherd replied, "nor think nor dare to know that which I know."

He said to Prince Florizel, "Sir! You have undone a man who is 83 years old. I thought that I would go peacefully to my grave and even die in the same bed in which my father died, and then lie close by his honest bones, but now some hangman must put on my shroud and lay me in a grave in which no priest shovels in dust. I will not receive a Christian burial."

He said to Perdita, "Oh, cursed wretch, who knew that this man was the Prince, and dared to be engaged to him! Undone! Undone! If I might die within this hour, I would have lived long enough to die when I desire."

The old shepherd departed.

Florizel said to the disguised Camillo, "Why are you looking that way at me? I am sorry that this has happened, but I am not afraid. My intention of being married to Perdita is delayed, but my intention has not changed. What I was, I still am. I am like a dog who strains to go forward, resisting the leash that is trying to pull him back; I am not following my leash, even unwillingly."

Camillo said, "My gracious lord, you know your father's temper. At this time he will allow no speech about you marrying this shepherdess, and I guess that you do not intend to talk to him. I also think that he will hardly endure your sight now and for a while, I fear. Therefore, until the fury of his Highness settles, do not see him."

"I do not intend to," Florizel said.

He looked closer at the disguised Camillo and said, "I think that you are … Camillo?"

"I am he, my lord," Camillo replied as he removed his false beard.

Perdita said to Florizel, "How often have I told you that this would happen! How often have I said that my being your beloved would last only until your father found out about it!"

"Our engagement cannot fail except by me violating my faith and my word," Florizel said, "and if that ever happens then let Nature crush the sides of the Earth together and destroy all the seeds of generation on Earth! Let all life end!

"Lift up your head, Perdita, and look more cheerfully. My father can take away my succession as King, if he wishes. What I wish to acquire is you. I prefer love of a woman to love of a crown."

"Be advised," Camillo said.

He meant, "Be careful," but Florizel pretended that he had meant, "Be counseled."

Florizel said, "I am being counseled, and by my fancy — my true love. If my reason will obey my love, then I will have reason and be sane. If not, then my senses, being better pleased with madness, will bid it welcome. If I cannot have my love, I will go insane."

"This is desperate, sir," Camillo replied.

"Call it desperate if you want," Florizel said, "but since it fulfills the vow I made to Perdita, I must call it honesty. Camillo, I will not break my oath to Perdita, my fair beloved, for Bohemia, or for the pomp that may be gleaned there, nor for all the Sun sees or all that the Earth holds enclosed within its womb or the profound sea hides in unknown fathoms. Therefore, I ask you, since you have always been my father's honored friend, that when he shall learn that I am gone — as, truly, I do not intend to see him any more — to give him good advice during his anger. Let fortune and me fight it out to determine my future. This you may know and so tell my father: I am going to sea with Perdita, whom I cannot hold on to and love on the shore of Bohemia. Fortunately for us, I have a vessel anchored nearby, but unfortunately for us it is not prepared for this plan. What course I mean to hold you need not know, and I will not tell you."

"Oh, my lord!" Camillo said. "I wish that your spirit were more inclined to listen to my advice, or more focused on what you need!"

"Listen, Perdita," Florizel said. He added to Camillo, "I'll talk to you in a moment." Florizel and Perdita talked together quietly.

Camillo said to himself, "He has made up his mind and won't change it. He has resolved to flee from his father and Bohemia. Now I would be happy if I could make his going from Bohemia do these things: serve my needs, save him from danger, show him respect and honor, and allow me to see again my dear Sicily and that unhappy King Leontes, my master, whom I so much thirst to see."

Florizel said, "Now, good Camillo, we can talk. I am so weighed down with business that requires my careful attention that I am forgetting my manners and ignoring you."

"Sir, I think that you have heard of my poor services that I have done for your father because of my respect for him."

"You have given my father very noble service and you have deserved very noble recompense," Florizel said. "It is my father's music to speak about your deeds, and he takes care to recompense them as you deserve."

"Well, my lord," Camillo said, "if you may please to think I love the King and through him love the person nearest to him, who is your gracious self, embrace my advice. If your more ponderous and settled project may suffer alteration, on my honor I'll point you to where you shall have such a reception as shall become your Highness. It will be a country where you may enjoy your betrothed, Perdita, from whom, I see, you will not be separated except — God forbid! — by your ruination. If you go to this country, you may marry her, and I will do my best in your absence to mollify your father and bring him to accept your marriage."

"How, Camillo, may this, which is almost a miracle, be done?" Florizel asked. "If you do this, I will call you something more than a man and afterward always have trust in you."

"Have you thought about the place where you will go to?" Camillo asked.

"Not yet," Florizel replied. "We did not expect my father to discover our engagement, and because it was discovered we must take action without preparation — we acknowledge that we are the slaves of chance and that every wind may blow us where it pleases."

"Then listen to me," Camillo said. "If you will not change your mind and stay in Bohemia, and if you insist on fleeing from your father, then sail to Sicily and present yourself and your Princess, as I see that she will become, before King Leontes. Perdita shall be dressed as becomes the partner of your bed. I think I can foretell that King Leontes will freely open his arms and weep as he welcomes you. He will ask you, King Polixenes' son, for forgiveness, as if you were your father. He will kiss the hands of your young and lively Princess. Again and again King Leontes will talk about his repentance for the unkindness he showed to your father and about the kindness and affection that he feels now for your father and you. He will chide to Hell his unkindness and will bid his kindness to grow faster than thought or time."

"Worthy Camillo, what reason for my visit shall I tell King Leontes?"

"Tell him that you were sent by King Polixenes, your father, to greet him and to give him comfort. Sir, I shall write down how you will behave toward King Leontes and the information that you will say your father told you to tell him. I know things that are known only by King Polixenes, King Leontes, and me, and I will write them down for you. That will let you know the things you should say when you meet with King Leontes. That way, he will think that you have your father's permission to be at his court and that you are telling him things that your father wants him to know."

"I am bound to you," Florizel said. "Some sense is in this."

"This course of action is more promising than a wild abandoning of yourselves to uncharted waters and undreamed-of shores. That course is very certain to bring you miseries enough, with no hope to help you, for as soon as you shake off one misery you will take on another. Your course of action is in no way as certain as your anchors, which at best can keep you in a place where you will hate to be. Besides, as you know, prosperity is what keeps love whole; affliction alters love's fresh complexion and heart."

"One of these is true," Perdita said. "I think that affliction may alter for the worse one's complexion, but not alter one's heart and mind."

"Do you think so?" Camillo asked. He liked her comment. He added, "There shall not in your father's house be born another as wise as you for a very long time."

"My good Camillo," Florizel said, "Perdita is as above her breeding as she is below our birth. Her birth may be below that of a Prince, but her character is much above that of a peasant."

"I cannot say that it is a pity that she lacks education," Camillo said, "because she seems to be the superior of most people who teach."

"I beg your pardon, sir," Perdita said. "For your kind words I will blush my thanks."

"You are my prettiest Perdita," Florizel said, "but we are in a mess. It is as if we were standing on thorns!"

He added, "Camillo, you have been the preserver of my father, and now you are my preserver. You, the medicine and physician of our house, have saved the life of my father and are now saving my life. How can we carry out your plan? We are not equipped like the son of the King of Bohemia, nor shall we appear as such in Sicily until we find proper clothing and equipment."

"My lord," Camillo said, "fear not. I think you know that all my fortune and possessions still remain in Sicily. I will make sure that you will be as royally dressed and equipped as if I myself were you, a Prince. Let me talk to you a moment so that I can prove to you that you shall lack nothing."

They talked quietly.

Meanwhile, Autolycus, who thought that he was alone, walked to a spot near them and said to himself, "Ha, ha! What a fool Honesty is! And Trust, his sworn brother, is a very simple gentleman! I have sold all my trumpery. Not a counterfeit stone, not a ribbon, mirror, bag of sweet-smelling herbs, brooch, notebook, ballad, knife, tape, glove, shoelace, bracelet, ring made of horn remains to keep my pack from fasting — my pack is completely empty of merchandise.

"The peasants thronged to see who would buy first, as if my trinkets were sacred and brought a benediction to the buyer. Because of that, I was able to see whose purse or wallet was fattest. What I saw, I remembered, and I put it to my own good use. Clown, who lacks something that would make him a reasonable man, grew so in love with the wenches' song that he would not stir his feet until he had learned both the tune and the words; the singing so drew the rest of the herd to me that all their senses other than hearing melted away. You might have stolen someone's underwear because the wearer was paying so little attention to anything but the song. It was nothing to steal a moneybag that was hanging from someone's belt. I could have filed keys off of chains because the peasants had no hearing and no feeling except for my Sir Clown's song, and admiring the nonsense of it.

"Therefore, during this time of their lethargy I picked pockets and cut the strings of most of their bags filled with money to spend at the festival. If the old shepherd had not come in with a hubbub because of his daughter and the King's son and scared my pigeons away from my trap of trumpery, I would not have left a purse alive in the whole army."

Camillo said to Florizel, "No, that is not a good objection. My letters, by the means I told you about, will be in Sicily as soon as you arrive."

Florizel started to ask, "And those that you'll procure from King Leontes —"

Camillo finished for him, "— shall satisfy your father."

Perdita said to Camillo, "May good luck come to you! All that you have said seems reasonable and favorable."

Seeing Autolycus, Camillo said, "Who have we here? We'll make use of this man; we ought to omit nothing that may give us aid."

Camillo's plan was for Florizel and this man, Autolycus, to exchange clothing. That would help disguise Florizel's identity.

Autolycus heard them talking and, shaking with fear, said to himself, "If they have overheard me talking to myself just now, why, I will be hanged."

Camillo said, "How are you, good fellow? Why are you shaking? Do not be afraid, man. We mean no harm to you."

"I am a poor fellow, sir," Autolycus said.

"Continue to be poor," Camillo replied. "No one here will steal your poverty from you. Yet for the outside of your poverty — your clothing — we must make an exchange; therefore, take off your outer clothing now. You must realize that there's a necessity in it — we want you to exchange garments with this gentleman. Although the bargain is worst on his side — his clothing is better than yours — yet wait just a minute. Here is some money for you."

"I am a poor fellow, sir," Autolycus said.

He thought, *I know you well enough. I know who you are, and I know that you are planning a trick of some kind.*

Camillo said, "Please, hurry. The gentleman is half flayed — half undressed — already."

"Are you in earnest, sir?" Autolycus said. "Are you serious about this exchange of clothing?"

He thought, *I smell the trick of it.*

Florizel said, "Hurry, please."

"Indeed, you have paid me, but I cannot with conscience take it," Autolycus said.

"Unbuckle, unbuckle," Camillo said.

Florizel and Autolycus exchanged clothing. Florizel's clothing was much better than the clothing of Autolycus. Although Florizel's clothing was not as fancy as that of a Prince, it was fancy enough to be worn at a festival by a shepherd who owned much pastureland — the kind of person whom Florizel had pretended to be. Autolycus had spent much of the money he had stolen from Clown on trumpery to fill his peddler's pack.

Camillo said to Perdita, "Fortunate mistress — let my words be a prophecy that will come true for you! You must go into some shrubbery that will hide you so you can take off some of your exterior fancy clothing that you wore as Queen of the sheep-shearing festival. Take your sweetheart's hat and pluck it down over your brows, hide your face, take off your mantle, and, as much as you can, disguise the truth of your own appearance. Do this so that you may — for I am afraid of spying eyes — get onboard the ship without being seen."

The words "disguise the truth of your own appearance" were interesting. Perdita was dressed as if she were the Queen of the Festival — she was dressed as royalty — and in fact she was a Princess. The way she appeared to be was in fact what she really was.

Perdita said, "I see the play so lies that I must bear a part. I see that our plan requires that I hide my identity."

"Yes," Camillo said. "It is required."

He asked Florizel, "Are you ready now?"

Florizel said, "If I should happen to meet my father, he would not know that I am his son."

Camillo said, "You shall not wear a hat."

He took Florizel's hat and gave it to Perdita, saying, "Come, lady, come. This is for you."

He said to Autolycus, "Farewell, my friend."

"*Adieu*, sir," Autolycus said.

"Oh, Perdita," Florizel said, "we two have forgotten something! Let me speak to you."

While they talked together, Camillo said quietly to himself, "What I will do next shall be to tell King Polixenes about this escape and where Florizel and Perdita are bound. By doing that, I hope that I shall persuade the King to follow them. In his company, I shall once again see Sicily, for whose sight I have the longing of a woman. I want to see Sicily as strongly as a pregnant woman wants to eat strange foods."

Camillo was not intentionally betraying Florizel and Perdita. He believed that the two ought to arrive in Sicily in plenty of time for them to be married before King Polixenes arrived. If the two lovers were already lawfully married, King Polixenes would be much more likely to accept their marriage. Rough weather, however, could slow their journey.

"May Fortune speed us on our way!" Florizel said. "Thus we set out, Camillo, to go to the seashore."

"The swifter your speed, the better," Camillo replied.

Florizel, Perdita, and Camillo departed.

"I understand the business, and I hear it," Autolycus said to himself, "To have an open ear, a quick eye, and a nimble hand is necessary for a cutpurse; a good nose is also needed to smell out work for the other senses. I see that this is a time in which the unjust man thrives. What an exchange had this been even without booty! What booty is here with this exchange! I greatly benefited by this exchange of clothing, and I got some money in addition!

"Surely the gods this year are conspiring with us, and we may do anything extempore, without planning it in advance. The Prince himself is guilty of a piece of iniquity; he is stealing away from his father with his clog — Perdita — at his heels.

"If I thought it were a piece of honesty to tell King Polixenes what his son the Prince is doing, I would not do it. I am a knave, and I believe it to be more knavish to conceal what the Prince is doing. I will act in such a way that I am loyal to my profession."

The old shepherd and his son, Clown, walked toward Autolycus, but they did not see him.

Autolycus said to himself, "Let me move aside. I don't want them to see me now. Here is more matter for a hot brain to think about. Every lane's end, shop, church, court session, and hanging yield a careful man work. I may be able to benefit by eavesdropping on these two."

Clown said to his father, the old shepherd, "See, see — what a man you are now! You are in so much trouble! The only thing we can do is to tell the King that Perdita is a changeling; she is not of your flesh and blood. Instead, she is a child left by the fairies."

"Listen to me," the old shepherd said.

"No, *you* listen to me."

"Go on, then."

Clown said, "Because Perdita is not of your flesh and blood, your flesh and blood have not offended King Polixenes, and so your flesh and blood are not to be punished by him. Show King Polixenes those things you found around her when you found her when she was an infant. Show him those secret things, all but what she has with her — what she is wearing as Queen of the Sheep-shearing Festival. Once you do this, you need not fear being punished, I assure you. You can let the law go whistle."

"I will tell the King everything, every word, yes, and his son's pranks, too," the old shepherd said. "The Prince, I say, is no honest man, neither to his father nor to me — not when he attempts to make me the King's brother-in-law."

Of course, the old shepherd would have been the father of the King's daughter-in-law; he would not have been the King's brother-in-law.

Clown said, "Indeed, brother-in-law was the farthest-off relative you could have been to the King and then your blood had been the dearer by I know how much an ounce. By being related to King Polixenes, your blood would be more valuable than if you were just a simple shepherd."

Autolycus said to himself, sarcastically, "These puppies are very wise!"

"Well, let us go to the King," the old shepherd said. "There are things in this bundle that will make him wonder, think hard, and scratch his beard."

Autolycus said to himself, "This complaint may in some way be an impediment to the flight of my master: Prince Florizel. At least, he is my old master: I used to serve him."

"Pray heartily that King Polixenes is in the palace," Clown said.

"Though I am not naturally honest, I am so sometimes by chance," Autolycus said to himself. "Let me take off my peddler's disguise."

He removed his false beard and said, "How now, rustics! Where are you bound?"

The old shepherd and his son did not recognize Autolycus, who was now wearing fancy clothing as well as being beardless.

The old shepherd said, "We are going to the palace, if it is all right with your worship."

Autolycus asked for much information: "Tell me the business you have there, the nature of that bundle, the place of your dwelling, your names, your ages, what property you have, your upbringing, and anything else that is fit to be known."

"We are but plain fellows, sir," Clown said.

"That is a lie," Autolycus said. "You are rough and hairy. Tell me no lies. Lying becomes none but tradesmen, and they often give us soldiers the lie by giving us poor quality or short quantity ... no, wait — we pay them for their goods with stamped coins, not stabbing steel, so therefore they do not give us the lie; instead, they sell it."

"Your worship almost gave a lie," Clown said, "but fortunately you caught yourself and corrected yourself."

"Are you a courtier, if you don't mind my asking, sir?" the old shepherd asked.

"Whether I mind it or not, I am a courtier," Autolycus said. "Don't you see the air of the court in the clothing I am wearing? Doesn't my gait have in it the measure of the court? Doesn't your nose smell court-odor emanating from me? Don't I look down on your baseness because I am a member of the upper class? Do you think that because I am talking to you in order to learn your business that I am therefore no courtier? I am a courtier from top to bottom, and I am a courtier who will either push on or pluck back your business at the palace. And now I command you to tell me what business you have at the palace."

"My business, sir, is with King Polixenes," the old shepherd said.

"What advocate do you have to go to him?" Autolycus asked.

"I don't know what you mean, sir," the old shepherd replied.

Clown said to the old shepherd, "The court-word for 'advocate' is a pheasant. Say that you don't have one."

Clown thought that "advocate" meant "influence." One way to influence a judge of a local court was with a bribe. A common bribe was poultry.

"None, sir," the old shepherd said. "I have no pheasant, rooster, or hen."

"How blessed are we who are not simple men!" Autolycus said proudly. "Yet nature might have made me as these are. Therefore I will not look down on them."

Autolycus was talking much like the Pharisee in Luke 18:9-14:

"He [Jesus] spake also this parable unto certain which trusted in themselves that they were just, and despised others.

"Two men went up into the Temple to pray: the one a Pharisee, and the other a Publican.

"The Pharisee stood and prayed thus with himself, 'O God, I thank thee that I am not as other men, extortioners, unjust, adulterers, or even as this Publican.

"'I fast twice in the week: I give tithe of all that ever I possess.'

"But the Publican standing afar off, would not lift up so much as his eyes to Heaven, but smote his breast, saying, 'Oh, God, be merciful to me, a sinner.'

"I tell you, this man departed to his house, justified rather than the other: for every man that exalteth himself shall be brought low, and he that humbleth himself shall be exalted."

Autolycus began to pick his teeth with a toothpick. This was a recent fashionable activity among the upper class.

Clown said to his father, "This man cannot be anything but a great courtier."

"His garments are rich, but he does not wear them well," the old shepherd said.

Fancy clothing is uncomfortable for those who are not accustomed to wear it and for those whom it does not fit.

"He seems to be all the more noble in being eccentric," Clown said. "He is a great man, I promise you. I know that because he picks his teeth."

"What is in that bundle you are carrying?" Autolycus asked. "Why are you carrying that box?"

The old shepherd replied, "Sir, secrets lie in this bundle and box that no one but the King must know, and he shall know those secrets within this hour, if I may come into his presence and talk to him."

"Old man, you have lost your labor," Autolycus said. "That will not happen."

"Why, sir?"

Autolycus, thinking quickly of a plan, lied, "The King is not at the palace; he has gone aboard a new ship to purge his melancholy and get fresh air for himself. If you are capable of knowing serious things, you must know that the King is full of grief."

"So it is said, sir," the old shepherd said. "He grieves that his son wanted to have married a shepherd's daughter."

"If that shepherd is not under arrest, let him flee from here," Autolycus said. "If he is arrested, the curses he shall have and the tortures he shall feel will break the back of a man and the heart of a monster."

"Do you think so, sir?" Clown asked.

"Not the old shepherd alone shall suffer whatever heavy and bitter vengeance ingenuity can make, but those who are related to the old shepherd, even if they are distantly related and removed fifty times, shall also all come under the jurisdiction of the hangman. Although it is a great pity, yet it is necessary. This old sheep-whistling rogue — this ram-tender — attempted to have his daughter become a member of the nobility by marrying Prince Florizel! Some say the old shepherd shall be stoned, but that death is too soft for him, in my opinion. He attempted to drag our country's throne into a shelter for sheep — a sheepcote! For him, all deaths are too few, and the sharpest death is too easy."

"Has the old man a son, sir?" Clown asked. "Have you heard whether he has a son, sir?"

"He does have a son, who shall be flayed alive," Autolycus said. "Then honey will be poured over him and he will be set on the top of a wasp's nest, and then he will be forced to stand until he is three quarters and a little bit more dead. After that, he will be revived with strong drink, and as raw as he is at that time, on the hottest day the almanac forecasts, he shall be set against a brick wall, with the Sun shining on him from the South, and the Sun shall see him swollen because of horsefly bites.

"But why are we talking about these traitorous rascals, whose miseries are to be smiled at because their offences are so great?" Autolycus said. "Tell me, for you seem to be honest plain men, what business you have with King Polixenes. For a consideration, aka bribe, I will take you to the ship where he is onboard. I will take you into his presence, and I will whisper to him and plead on your behalf. If it is possible for any man other than the King to accomplish your purposes, I am the man who can do it."

Clown said to his father, "He seems to be very powerful. Make a deal with him, and give him gold. Although a powerful person can be a stubborn bear, with the gift of gold, one can often lead a powerful person by the nose. Show the inside of your wallet to the outside of his hand, and we can solve our problem. Remember 'stoned,' and 'flayed alive.'"

"If it please you, sir, to undertake the business for us, here is the gold I have on me," the old shepherd said to Autolycus. "I'll give you as much more as this and leave this young man as security until I bring you the additional gold."

"After I have done what I promised to do?" Autolycus asked.

"Yes, sir."

"Well, give me the gold you have on you," Autolycus said.

He then asked Clown, "Are you a party in this business?"

"In some way I am, sir," Clown replied, "but although my case is a pitiful one, I hope I shall not be flayed out of it."

Clown was punning. A case is a situation that law enforcement officers investigate, and a case or a casing is a covering. Clown's body was covered with skin.

"Oh, that's the case of the shepherd's son," Autolycus said. "Hang him; he'll be made an example to others."

Clown said to his father, "Take comfort, good comfort! We have a plan. We must go to the King and show him our strange sights — this bundle and box. King Polixenes must know that Perdita is not your daughter nor my sister; we are done for otherwise."

Clown said to Autolycus, "Sir, I will give you as much as this old man does when the business is performed, and I will remain with you, as he said, as your security until the gold is brought to you."

"I will trust you," Autolycus said. "Walk ahead of me and go toward the seashore. Go on the right. I will look upon the hedge and follow you."

"Look upon the hedge" was a euphemism for "urinate."

Clown said to his father, "We are blessed that we met this man — yes, we are blessed."

"Let's walk ahead of him as he asked us to," the old shepherd said. "God sent him to us so he could do us good."

The old shepherd and his son walked away.

While urinating, Autolycus said to himself, "If I had a mind to be honest, I see that Fortune would not allow me to be honest. She drops rewards in my mouth. I am presented now with a double opportunity: gold and a means to do my former master Prince Florizel good. Who knows how this may turn out to be to my advantage?

"I will bring these two moles, these blind ones, onboard the ship that Prince Florizel is on. If he thinks it fit to put them on shore again and if he thinks that the information they want to present to the King does not concern him, let him call me a rogue for being so officious. I am impervious against that insult and the shame that goes with it. I will present these two men to him; there may be something good in it for me."

CHAPTER 5
— 5.1 —

In a room of the palace in Sicily, King Leontes, Cleomenes, Dion, and Paulina were speaking. Some gentlemen were also present. Cleomenes and Dion were the two lords whom King Leontes had sent to consult the oracle of Apollo sixteen years earlier.

Cleomenes said to King Leontes, "Sir, you have done enough; you have performed a saint-like penitence. No sin could you have committed that you have not redeemed; indeed, you have paid down more penitence than you have done trespass. Now, finally, do as the Heavens have done: Forget your sins, and with them forgive yourself."

"While I remember Hermione and her virtues," King Leontes said, "I cannot forget my blemishes in comparison to her virtues, and so I continually think of the wrong I myself did, which was so great that it has made my Kingdom heirless and destroyed the sweetest companion who ever gave a man hope for the future."

"That is true, too true, my lord," Paulina said. "If, one by one, you wedded all the women in the world, or from each of the women who exist took something good in order to make a perfect woman, the woman — Hermione — you killed would still be unparalleled."

"I think so, too," King Leontes said. "Killed! The woman I killed! I did kill her, but you strike and hurt me sorely, when you say I killed her; it is as bitter upon your tongue as in my thoughts. Now, please, say only seldom that I killed her."

Cleomenes said to Paulina, "It is best not to say it at all, good lady. You might have spoken a thousand things that would have been more beneficial and kinder."

"You are one of those people who want King Leontes to get a new wife," Paulina replied.

"If you don't want the King to remarry," Dion said, "you don't pity the state, nor the continuance of the King's most sovereign name. King Leontes — and Sicily — needs a royal heir. You are not thinking about what dangers, because his Highness has no living heir, may drop upon his Kingdom and devour citizens who are not sure what to do. What is more holy than to rejoice that the former Queen is well in Heaven? What would be holier than — for the sake of the King and Sicily, for our present comfort, and for our future good — to bless the bed of majesty again with a sweet spouse in it?"

"There is none worthy to grace the bed of the King," Paulina said. "None is worthy when compared with the Queen who is gone. Besides, the gods must have their secret purposes fulfilled. Has not the divine Apollo said, and is it not the tenor of his oracle, that King Leontes shall not have an heir until his lost child — his daughter — is found? But that his daughter shall be found is altogether as unnatural from the point of view of our human reason as it would be for my husband, Antigonus, to break out of his grave and come again to me. Antigonus, I swear on my life, perished with the infant. It is your counsel that King Leontes should be contrary to the Heavens and oppose the will of the gods."

Paulina then said to King Leontes, "Don't worry about having an heir. The crown will find an heir. Remember that Alexander the Great left his crown to the worthiest; that way, his successor was likely to be the best."

"Good Paulina, who I know honors the memory of Hermione," King Leontes said, "I wish that I had always obeyed your counsel! If I had, even now I might have looked upon my Queen's full, not hollow, eyes, have taken treasure from her lips —"

"— and left them richer for what they yielded," Paulina said.

"You speak the truth," King Leontes said. "There are no more such wives; therefore, there is no wife for me. A wife worse than Paulina, and better treated by me, would make her sainted spirit once again possess her corpse, and on this stage, where I would stand, offending her, she would appear soul-vexed, and begin, 'Why are you insulting me by treating better than you treated me a wife who is worse than me?'"

"Had she such power, she would have just cause to do that," Paulina said.

"She would have," King Leontes said, "and she would provoke me to murder the new wife I married."

"I would do the same thing," Paulina said. "Were I the ghost who walked, I would tell you to look at your new wife's eyes, and then I would ask you to tell me because of what dull part in them you chose to make her your wife, and then I would shriek so that your ears would split to hear me, and the words that would follow the shriek would be 'Remember my eyes.'"

"Her eyes were stars, stars," King Leontes said, "and all other eyes else were dead coals! You need fear no wife. I will have no wife, Paulina."

"Will you swear never again to marry except with my freely given permission?" Paulina asked.

"I swear," King Leontes said, "on my immortal soul!"

"Then, my good lords," Paulina said, "bear witness to his oath."

"You tempt him to swear to follow the wrong path," Cleomenes said. "He should not swear this oath."

"He shall not marry unless another woman, as like Hermione as is her picture, appears in front of his eyes," Paulina replied.

"Good madam —" Cleomenes began.

"I am finished," Paulina said to him.

She then said to King Leontes, "Yet, if my lord does marry again — if you will, sir; I make no promise, but if you do — give me the duty of choosing a Queen for you. She shall not be as young as was your former Queen, but she shall be such as, if your first Queen's ghost should walk on this Earth, it should feel joy if it saw her in your arms."

Using the royal plural, King Leontes said, "My true Paulina, we shall not marry until you allow us."

"That shall be when your first Queen is alive again," Paulina said. "You shall not remarry until that happens."

A gentleman entered the room and said, "A man who says that he is Prince Florizel, son of King Polixenes of Bohemia, along with his Princess, the most beautiful woman whom I have ever seen, desires to speak to your Highness."

"Who is with him?" King Leontes asked. "He has not come here in a manner befitting his father's greatness. His approach, so lacking in ceremony and so sudden, tells us that this is not a planned visit, but has been forced on him by need and accident. What train of followers does he have with him?"

"He has very few followers, and those are lower class," the gentleman replied.

"Did you say his Princess is with him?"

"Yes, she is the most peerless mortal piece of earth, I think, that the Sun has ever shone brightly on."

"Oh, Hermione," Paulina said, "as every present time boasts itself to be better than a better age that has passed, so must your grave give way to what's seen now! This living Princess is being called more beautiful than you, my late Queen!"

She said to the gentleman, "Sir, you yourself have spoken and written about Queen Hermione's beauty, but your writing now is colder than that theme. You wrote about her, 'She had not been, nor ever was to be equaled.' Your verse flowed with her beauty once: it is shrewdly ebbed now that you say that you have seen a better woman than Hermione."

"Please pardon me, madam," the gentleman said. "I have almost forgotten Hermione — I beg your pardon — but this new woman, when you see her, will have your praises, too. This is a creature who, if she were to begin a religious sect, might quench the zeal of all followers of other religions, and make proselytes of everyone whom she asked to follow her."

"Men, perhaps, but not women," Paulina scoffed.

"Women will love her because she is a woman more worthy than any man," the gentleman said. "Men will love her because she is the rarest of all women."

"Go, Cleomenes," King Leontes ordered. "You, assisted with your honored friends, will bring them here so that we can welcome them. Still, it is strange that Prince Florizel should visit us without previous notification."

Cleomenes and a few other gentlemen departed.

Paulina said, "If our Prince Mamillius, that jewel of children, had seen this hour, he would be much like this lord. There is not even a month's difference in the time of their births."

She had heard about Prince Florizel, although she had not yet seen him.

"Please, say no more about Mamillius," King Leontes said. "Cease talking about him. You know that he dies to me again when I hear him talked about. I am sure that when I shall see this gentleman, your speeches will make me think about my son's death, and that may take away my reason."

He looked up and said, "Here they come."

Cleomenes and the other gentlemen escorted Prince Florizel and Perdita into the room and the presence of King Leontes.

King Leontes said, "Prince Florizel, we know that your mother was completely true to her husband because she made an exact copy of your royal father when she conceived and gave birth to you. If I were twenty-one years old again, your father's image is so stamped in you — his exact appearance, manner, and bearing! — that I would call you brother, as I did him, and speak about some wild deed that he and I did together.

"You are very dearly welcome! And your fair Princess — she is a goddess! Sadly, I lost a couple — my wife and my son — who between Heaven and Earth might have stood begetting wonder as you and your Princess, a gracious couple, do. I also lost — through my own folly — the society and the friendship of your splendid father, whom, although my life is miserable, I hope to live long enough to once more see."

Prince Florizel said, "By my father's command, I have here landed on Sicily and from him I give you all greetings that a King, in friendship, can send his brother. Except that the infirmity that attends old age has somewhat seized hold of and taken away some of the ability he wishes he had, he himself would have traveled the lands and waters that lie between your throne and his so that he could see you, whom he loves — he told me to tell you this — more than all living Kings who bear scepters."

"Oh, King Polixenes, my brother, you good gentleman!" King Leontes said. "The wrongs I have done you stir afresh within me, and these your official friendly greetings, which are so wonderfully kind, show me that I have been remiss in not sending you such friendly greetings.

"You, Prince Florizel, are as welcome here as is the spring to the Earth. And King Polixenes has also exposed this paragon — your Princess — to the fearful, or at least, rough treatment of the dreadful Neptune, god of the seas, to greet a man not worth her trouble, much less the risk of her life."

"My good lord," Prince Florizel said, "my Princess came from Libya."

"Isn't Libya where the warlike Smalus, that noble and honored lord, is feared and loved?" King Leontes asked.

"Yes, most royal sir, she came from there," Prince Florizel said. "When she parted from him, his tears proclaimed that she was his daughter. From Libya, a friendly and helpful south wind helped us sail here so we could obey the order my father gave me to visit your Highness. I have sent away from your Sicilian shores the best part of my train of followers. They are heading for Bohemia to tell my father the good news of my success in getting a wife from Libya and the good news that my wife and I have safely arrived in Sicily."

"May the blessed gods purge all disease from our air while you stay here!" King Leontes said. "You have a holy father, a graceful gentleman, against whose person, as sacred as it is, I have sinned, for which the Heavens, taking angry note of my sin, have left me without a child. In contrast, your father is blessed — and he deserves to be blessed by Heaven — with you, who are worthy of his goodness.

"I wish that I had acted differently so that now I might have a son and daughter to look on — a son and daughter as good as you!"

A lord entered the room and said, "Most noble sir, that which I shall report would not be believed if the proof of it were not so near. If it should please you, great sir, King Polixenes of Bohemia greets you from himself by me. He wants you to arrest his son, who has — casting aside his dignity as a Prince and his duty as a son — fled from his father, from his hopes of inheriting the crown, and with a shepherd's daughter."

"Where's the King of Bohemia?" King Leontes asked. "Tell me."

"He is here in your city," the lord said. "I just now came from him. I speak amazedly; and my confused speech is suitable for my wonderment and my message. While he was hurrying to your court, chasing, it seems, this fair couple here, he met on the way the father of this woman — who has the appearance of a lady — and her brother, both of whom fled from their country with this young Prince."

"Camillo has betrayed me," Florizel said, "although his honor and honesty until now endured all weathers. Never before has he betrayed me."

The lord said, "You will be able to charge him with that. He's with the King, your father."

"Who? Camillo?" King Leontes asked.

"Yes, Camillo, sir," the lord said. "I spoke with him; he is now interrogating these two poor men whom I mentioned. I have never seen wretches so quake in fear like them. They kneel, and they kiss the earth; they perjure and contradict themselves as often as they speak. The King of Bohemia stops his ears, and he threatens them with different ways of torturing them to death."

"Oh, my poor father!" Perdita said. "The immortal gods have set informers upon us. The immortal gods will not allow us to be formally married."

"Are you formally married?" King Leontes asked.

"We are not, sir, nor are we likely to be," Prince Florizel replied. "The stars, I see, will kiss the valleys first. The odds of a high-born person marrying a low-born person are the same as that of all the stars kissing the valleys."

"My lord," King Leontes asked, "is this woman the daughter of a King?"

"She is," Prince Florizel replied, "when once she is my wife."

"That 'once' I see by your good father's speed will come on very slowly," King Leontes said. "I am sorry, very sorry, you have displeased him and ignored your duty to obey him, and I am as sorry that your choice to be your wife is not as rich in birth as she is in beauty. If she were, then you might very well enjoy her."

Prince Florizel said to Perdita, "Dear, look up and cheer up. Although Lady Fortune, who is clearly an enemy to us, should chase us with my father, she has no power at all to change our love for each other."

He then said to King Leontes, "I beg you, sir, remember when you were as young as I am now. Remember the love that you felt then, and step forth and be my advocate. At your request, my father will grant precious things as if they were trifles."

"If he would do so," King Leontes said, "I would beg to be given your precious woman here, whom he considers to be only a trifle."

"Sir, my liege," Paulina said, "your eye has too much youth in it. Not a month before your Queen died, she was worthier of such gazes of admiration than the woman you look on now."

"I was thinking of my late Queen even as I gazed at this woman," King Leontes replied.

He said to Prince Florizel, "But I have not yet answered your petition. I will do that now. I will go to your father. As long as your honor is not overthrown by your desires — as long as you do not have premarital sex with this woman — I am a friend to your desires and to you. I now go to your father as your advocate; therefore, follow me and see what progress I make as your advocate. Come, my good lord."

Autolycus and a gentleman talked together in front of King Leontes' palace.

Autolycus asked the gentleman, "Please tell me, sir, if you were present at this narration of events."

"I was present at the opening of the old shepherd's bundle, and I heard the old shepherd tell the manner of how he found it. After a period of amazedness, we were all ordered out of the chamber. One more thing I thought I heard the shepherd say is that he found the child."

"I would very gladly know what else happened," Autolycus said.

"I can give you only an incomplete account of what happened," the gentleman replied, "but the changes I perceived in King Leontes and Camillo were exclamation marks of admiration. They seemed almost, with staring at one another, to tear the lids of their eyes — it was as if their eyes were starting out of their heads. Speech was in their dumbness, and language in their very gestures; they looked as if they had heard of a world ransomed, or one destroyed. A notable passion of wonder appeared in them, but the wisest beholder, who knew no more than what he saw, could not say if the meaning were joy or sorrow, but it had to be one or the other to an extreme degree. They were either very happy or filled with much sorrow."

Another gentleman arrived, and the first gentleman said, "Here comes a gentleman who perhaps knows more than I know."

He asked the newly arrived gentleman, "What is the news, Rogero?"

Rogero replied, "We can see nothing but bonfires everywhere in celebration of the news: The oracle is fulfilled because the King's daughter has been found. Such a deal of wonder is broken out within this hour that ballad-makers will not be able to express it."

A third gentleman arrived, and Rogero said, "Here comes the Lady Paulina's steward; he can tell you more."

Rogero said to the third gentleman, "How goes it now, sir? This news that is called true is so like an old tale that the truth of it is in strong suspicion. Has the King truly found his heir?"

"That is very true," the third gentleman said, "if truth ever were made pregnant — filled out — by circumstantial evidence. That which you hear you'll swear you see because there is such consistency in the evidence. The mantle of Queen Hermione's, her jewel on the mantle's neck, the letters of Antigonus found with it that are known to be in his handwriting, the majesty of the daughter in her resemblance to her mother, the quality of nobleness that her nature shows above her upbringing, and many other evidences proclaim Perdita with all certainty to be the King's daughter. Did you see the meeting of the two Kings: Leontes and Polixenes?"

Rogero replied, "No."

"Then you have lost a sight, which needed to be seen, as speaking is not sufficient to convey it. At the two Kings' meeting, you might have beheld one joy crown another, so and in such manner that it seemed sorrow wept to take leave of them, for their joy waded in tears. The Kings cast up their eyes and held up their hands, and their countenances were so distorted by their emotion that the two Kings had to be distinguished by their clothing rather than by their faces. Our King, who was ready to leap out of his skin because of his joy at finding his daughter, as if that joy had now become a loss, cried, 'Oh, your mother, your mother!' Then he asked the King of Bohemia for forgiveness, then he embraced his son-in-law, and then again he vehemently embraced his daughter. Next he thanked the old shepherd, who stood by like a weather-bitten conduit of many Kings' reigns — the old shepherd looked like a gargoyle from whose mouth rainwater pours. I never heard of such another encounter, which lames any report that tries to follow it and undoes any description that tries to describe it."

"Can you tell me, please, what became of Antigonus, who carried the child away from here?" Rogero asked.

"That is like an old tale still, which will have content to relate, although everyone has stopped believing the tale and no one is listening to it. Antigonus was torn to pieces by a bear. The shepherd's son witnessed this. He has not only his innocence and guilelessness, of which he seems to have much, to justify him, but he also has a handkerchief and rings that Paulina recognized as belonging to Antigonus."

The first gentleman asked, "What became of Antigonus' ship and his followers?"

"They were shipwrecked at the same instant of their master's death and in the view of the old shepherd's son so that all the people who helped to expose the child were lost at the moment when it was found. But a noble combat between joy and sorrow was fought in Paulina! She had one eye declined because her husband has been confirmed to be dead, and the other eye elevated because the oracle has been fulfilled; she wept with one eye and laughed with the other. Paulina lifted Princess Perdita from the earth, and so locked her in her hug that it was as if she wanted to pin her to her heart so that she might never again be in danger of being lost."

The first gentleman said, "The dignity and excellence of this scene were worth the audience of Kings and Princes; for by such was it acted."

The third gentleman said, "One of the prettiest touches of all was some angling that caught the water — my tears — although not the fish of my eyes. During the telling of the Queen's death, with the manner how she came to it bravely confessed and lamented by King Leontes, his daughter, who paid close attention, was wounded. She made one sign of dolor after another, and with a sign of mourning she — I dare say — bled tears. I am sure that my own heart wept blood. Whoever was most marble there changed color; even those who were the most hard-hearted melted. Some fainted, and all sorrowed. If everyone in the world could have seen it, the woe would have been universal."

"Have they returned to the court?" the first gentleman asked.

"No," the third gentleman replied. "The Princess heard about her mother's statue, which is in the keeping of Paulina. The statue is a masterpiece many years in the making and has been just now completed by that talented Italian master Julio Romano, who, if he had eternity and could put breath into his work, would take away from Nature her job of creating living human beings, so perfectly is he her imitator. He has made his statue so closely resemble Hermione that they say a person would speak to the statue and wait in expectation of an answer. They have eagerly gone to see the statue, and there they intend to dine."

The second gentleman said, "I thought that Paulina had some great matter going on there because she has privately twice or thrice a day, ever since the death of Hermione, visited that remote house. Shall we go there and add our company to the rejoicing?"

The first gentleman said, "Who would be anywhere else if he had the benefit of access? With every wink of an eye some new grace will be born. Our absence makes us unthrifty to our knowledge — we are wasting an opportunity to add to our knowledge. Let's go."

The gentlemen departed.

Alone, Autolycus said, "Now, if I did not have a dash of my former life in me, good things would drop on my head. I brought the old shepherd and his son aboard the Prince's ship, and I told him that I had heard them talk about a bundle and I know not what. Unfortunately, the shepherd's daughter, as the Prince then thought her to be, although he was overly fond of her, began to be very seasick, and the Prince was almost as seasick, and so the solution of this mystery remained undiscovered. But it is all one to me. Even if I had been the finder out of this secret, it would not have been appreciated because of my many criminal actions."

The old shepherd and Clown walked toward Autolycus. They were dressed in the clothing of gentlemen.

Autolycus said, "Here come those I have done good to against my will; they are already appearing in the blossoms of their good fortune."

"Come, boy," the old shepherd said. "I am past fathering more children, but your sons and daughters will be all gentlemen born."

This was not quite accurate — daughters cannot be gentlemen. In addition, a gentleman born has to have had three generations of nobility on both sides — the paternal and the maternal. The old shepherd's grandchildren — Clown's children — would most likely have three generations only on the paternal side.

Clown said to Autolycus, "You are well met, sir. You declined to fight with me the other day because I was not a gentleman born. Do you see these clothes? Say to me that you do not see them and that you still think that I am not a gentleman born. You had best say that these robes are not gentlemen born. Give me the lie, do, and try whether I am not now a gentleman born. As a gentleman, I must fight anyone who says that I am lying and that I am not a gentleman."

"I know you are now, sir, a gentleman born," Autolycus replied.

"Yes, and I have been a gentleman born for these last four hours," Clown said.

"And so have I, boy," the old shepherd said.

"So you have, but I was a gentleman born before my father because the King's son took me by the hand, and called me brother first," Clown said, "and then the two Kings called my father brother; and then the Prince my brother and the Princess my sister called my father, father; and so we wept, and those were the first gentleman-like tears that ever we shed."

"We may live, son, to shed many more."

"Yes, or else it would be hard luck, being in so preposterous estate as we are."

Clown meant that they were in a *prosperous* state, but "preposterous" seems more apt.

"I humbly ask you, sir," Autolycus said, "to pardon all the faults I have committed to your worship and to give a good report about me to the Prince my master."

"Please do, son," the old shepherd said. "We must be gentle now that we are gentlemen."

The old shepherd's notion of gentlemen was that they are generous.

"Will you amend your life?" Clown asked Autolycus.

"Yes, if your worship wants me to."

"Give me your hand," Clown said. "I will swear to the Prince that you are as honest and true a fellow as any fellow is in Bohemia."

"You may say it, but do not swear it," the old shepherd said.

"Not swear it, now I am a gentleman?" Clown said. "Let peasants and farmers say it, I'll swear it."

"Suppose that you swear to something that is false, son?"

"Even if it is false, a true gentleman may swear it on behalf of his friend," Clown replied.

He said to Autolycus, "I'll swear to the Prince that you are a brave fellow and good with weapons and that you will not be drunk; but I know that you are not a brave fellow and are not good with weapons and that you will be drunk. Nevertheless, I'll swear it, and I wish that you were a brave fellow and good with weapons."

"I will try to be one to the best of my ability," Autolycus said.

"Yes, by any means prove that you are a brave fellow," Clown said. "If I do not wonder how you can dare to be drunk when you are not a brave fellow, then do not trust me. Listen! King Polixenes and King Leontes, and the Prince and the Princess, our kindred, are going to see the Queen's image. Come and follow us — we'll be your good advocates."

In the chapel of Paulina's house were King Leontes, King Polixenes, Prince Florizel, Princess Paulina, some lords, and some attendants.

King Leontes said, "Oh, dignified and good Paulina, I have received great comfort from you!"

"Sovereign sir, I have always meant well even if sometimes I have not done well. All my services you have paid for in full, but you are more than gracious when, with your crowned brother — King Polixenes — and these your engaged heirs — Prince Florizel and Princess Perdita — of your Kingdoms, you visit my poor house. This is an honor that I will never be able to repay you."

"Oh, Paulina," King Leontes said, "we are giving you the trouble of hosting us, but we came to see the statue of our Queen. We have passed through your art gallery, which has many notable artworks, but we have not seen the artwork that my daughter came to look upon: the statue of her mother."

Paulina replied, "As she lived peerless, so her dead likeness, I do well believe, excels whatever yet you looked upon or the hand of man has done; therefore, I keep it lonely, apart from the other artworks. But here it is, in my chapel. Prepare to see life as closely imitated as ever still sleep has imitated death. Look at it, and say it is well created."

Paulina drew a curtain and revealed the artwork. All were silent as they looked at the statue of Hermione.

Paulina said, "I like your silence; it very much shows your wonder. However, you should speak. First, you, my liege, don't you think that it comes very near to life?"

King Leontes said, "This is Hermione's natural posture! Criticize me, dear stone, so that I may say indeed you are Hermione. Or rather, you are she in that you are not criticizing me because Hermione was as tender and gentle as infancy and grace. But, Paulina, Hermione was not as wrinkled as this statue is. She was not as old as this statue seems to be."

King Polixenes said, "Not as old by many years."

"This reveals the excellence of the sculptor," Paulina said. "He has sculpted Hermione as if sixteen years had passed. He has sculpted her as she would be if she were still alive today."

"The statue looks as she would look now if she were still alive," King Leontes said. "She would have added much to the quality of my life, and my soul is pierced because she is not alive. Oh, in life she stood like this statue. She had such life of majesty, warm life — but the statue coldly stands — when I first wooed her! I am ashamed. Doesn't the stone rebuke me for being more stone — in my heart — than it? Oh, royal sculptural masterpiece, there's magic in your majesty, which has conjured me to remember and has taken the ability to move from your daughter, Perdita, who is standing as still as stone, like you."

Perdita said, "Give me permission — and do not say that it is superstition — to kneel before this statue and implore her blessing."

She said to the statue, "Lady, dear Queen, whose life ended when my life had just began, give me that hand of yours to kiss."

"Be patient!" Paulina said. "Do not touch the statue. It has been newly set on the pedestal and newly painted — the paint is not dry."

Camillo said to King Leontes, "My lord, your sorrow was too sorely laid on you. The winds of sixteen winters cannot blow away your sorrow, and the Suns of sixteen summers cannot dry up your sorrow. Scarcely any joys have lasted that long, and all other sorrows have killed and ended themselves before that length of time."

"My dear brother," King Polixenes said to King Leontes, "let me, who was a cause of this, have permission to take off so much grief from you as I will bear myself. Let me share your sorrow and so relieve you of a part of it."

"Indeed, my lord," Paulina said to King Leontes, "if I had thought the sight of my poor image of Hermione would have so affected you — for the stone sculpture is mine — I would not have showed it to you."

She moved to draw the curtain shut.

King Leontes said, "Do not draw the curtain."

"You shall not look any longer at the statue," Paulina said, "lest your imagination make you think that the statue moves."

"Let it be so, let it happen," King Leontes said. "May I die if I don't already think that —"

He was going to say "the statue moves," but instead he asked, "— who was the sculptor who created this?"

He then asked King Polixenes, "Look at it, my lord. Wouldn't you say that the statue breathes — and that those veins do truly carry blood?"

"The statue is masterly created," King Polixenes said. "Life truly seems warm upon her lips."

King Leontes said, "The way that the eyes are set seem to make them move. Art is mocking us by making us think that art is life."

"I'll draw the curtain," Paulina said. "My lord is almost so far transported that he'll soon think that the statue is alive."

"Sweet Paulina, make me think that for the next twenty years!" King Leontes said. "No sane senses of the world can match the pleasure of the madness of thinking that this statue is alive. Let the curtain alone."

"I am sorry, sir, that I have thus far afflicted you, but I could afflict you farther," Paulina said.

"Do that, Paulina," King Leontes said, "because this affliction has a taste as sweet as any heart-warming drink. Still, I think, breath is coming from her. What fine chisel could ever cut breath? Let no man mock me, for I will kiss her."

"My good lord, don't kiss the statue," Paulina said. "The ruddiness upon her lips is wet paint. You'll mar the statue if you kiss it and stain your own lips with oily painting. Shall I draw the curtain?"

"No," King Leontes said. "Do not draw the curtain for the next twenty years."

"I could stand here for that long and look at this statue," Perdita said.

Paulina said, "Either stop and immediately leave this chapel, or prepare yourself to experience more amazement. If you can behold it, I'll make the statue truly move, descend from the pedestal, and take you by the hand; but then you'll think — which I protest is not true — that I am assisted by wicked powers."

King Leontes said, "What you can make her do, I will be happy to see. What you can make her speak, I will be happy to hear. It is as easy to make her speak as move."

"It is required that you awaken your faith," Paulina said. "Everyone stand still, and let's go on. Anyone who thinks that what I am about to do is unlawful business can depart."

"Proceed," King Leontes said. "No foot shall stir away from here."

Paulina said, "Music, wake her; begin to play!"

Music started to play.

Paulina said to the statue, "It is time; descend."

The statue, of course, did not move.

"Be stone no more."

The statue, of course, did not move.

"Approach."

The statue, of course, did not move.

"Strike all who look upon you with marvel and wonder."

The statue, of course, did not move.

"Come, and I'll fill your grave up."

The statue, of course, did not move.

"Move, and come here. Bequeath to death your numbness, because dear life redeems you from death."

The statue moved.

Paulina said, "You can see that she moves."

The living Hermione came down from the pedestal and went to King Leontes and held out her hand to him.

Paulina said to King Leontes, "Do not be startled. Her actions shall be as holy as you hear my spell is lawful. I am not practicing black magic. Do not shun her until you see her die again because if you shun her then you kill her twice. Do not hold back. Present your hand to her. When she was young, you wooed her; in old age is she now to become the suitor?"

King Leontes held her hand and said, "Oh, she's warm! If this is magic, let it be an art as lawful as eating."

King Polixenes said, "Hermione is embracing him."

Camillo said, "She is hanging on his neck. If she is alive, let her speak, too."

"Yes," King Polixenes said, "and tell us where she has been living — or how you stole her from the Land of the Dead."

"That she is alive," Paulina said, "you would scoff at if it were merely told to you as in an old tale, but you can see that she is alive, although she has not yet spoken. Wait a little while longer."

She said to Perdita, "It is your time to intervene, please, fair madam. Kneel and ask for your mother's blessing."

She said to Hermione, "Turn, good lady; our Perdita is found."

Hermione said, "You gods, look down and from your sacred vials pour your blessings upon my daughter's head! Tell me, my own daughter, where have you been preserved? Where have you lived? How did you come to your father's court? You shall hear that I, learning from Paulina that the oracle gave hope that you were still alive, have preserved myself so I could see you again."

"There's time enough for telling our stories," Paulina said. "Others may at this time interrupt your joy as they tell their own parts of the story. Go together, all you precious winners, and share your exultation with everyone. I, an old turtledove, will fly to some withered bough and there until I am dead I will lament my mate, who is dead and will never again be found."

"Be at peace, Paulina!" King Leontes said. "You should take a husband on my recommendation, as I have taken a wife on your recommendation. This is an agreement that was made between us by vows. You have found my wife, but how you found her is a question to be answered because I saw her, as I thought, dead, and I have in vain said many prayers upon her grave.

"I'll not seek far — as for him, I partly know his mind — to find you an honorable husband."

He then said, "Come, Camillo, and take Paulina by the hand. Her worth and honesty are very well known and here vouched for by Polixenes and me, a pair of Kings.

"Let's go from this place."

He then said to Hermione, who was uncertain how to act with King Polixenes, "What! Look upon my brother King. I beg both your pardons that ever I put between your holy and chaste looks my ill suspicion.

"This is Prince Florizel, your future son-in-law, and son of King Polixenes. Prince Florizel, as directed by the Heavens, is engaged to your daughter."

He then said, "Good Paulina, lead us away from here to some place where we may leisurely learn from each one which part he or she performed in this wide gap of time since first my wife and I were separated. Lead us hastily away."

Appendix A: About the Author

It was a dark and stormy night. Suddenly a cry rang out, and on a hot summer night in 1954, Josephine, wife of Carl Bruce, gave birth to a boy — me. Unfortunately, this young married couple allowed Reuben Saturday, Josephine's brother, to name their first-born. Reuben, aka "The Joker," decided that Bruce was a nice name, so he decided to name me Bruce Bruce. I have gone by my middle name — David — ever since.

Being named Bruce David Bruce hasn't been all bad. Bank tellers remember me very quickly, so I don't often have to show an ID. It can be fun in charades, also. When I was a counselor as a teenager at Camp Echoing Hills in Warsaw, Ohio, a fellow counselor gave the signs for "sounds like" and "two words," then she pointed to a bruise on her leg twice. Bruise Bruise? Oh yeah, Bruce Bruce is the answer!

Uncle Reuben, by the way, gave me a haircut when I was in kindergarten. He cut my hair short and shaved a small bald spot on the back of my head. My mother wouldn't let me go to school until the bald spot grew out again.

Of all my brothers and sisters (six in all), I am the only transplant to Athens, Ohio. I was born in Newark, Ohio, and have lived all around Southeastern Ohio. However, I moved to Athens to go to Ohio University and have never left.

At Ohio U, I never could make up my mind whether to major in English or Philosophy, so I got a bachelor's degree with a double major in both areas, then I added a Master of Arts degree in English and a Master of Arts degree in Philosophy. Yes, I have my MAMA degree.

Currently, and for a long time to come (I eat fruits and veggies), I am spending my retirement writing books such as *Nadia Comaneci: Perfect 10*, *The Funniest People in Dance*, *Homer's* Iliad: *A Retelling in Prose*, and *William Shakespeare's* Othello: *A Retelling in Prose*.

By the way, my sister Brenda Kennedy writes romances such as *A New Beginning* and *Shattered Dreams*.

Appendix B: Some Books by David Bruce

Retellings of a Classic Work of Literature

Arden of Faversham: *A Retelling*

Ben Jonson's The Alchemist: *A Retelling*

Ben Jonson's The Arraignment, or Poetaster: *A Retelling*

Ben Jonson's Bartholomew Fair: *A Retelling*

Ben Jonson's The Case is Altered: *A Retelling*

Ben Jonson's Catiline's Conspiracy: *A Retelling*

Ben Jonson's The Devil is an Ass: *A Retelling*

Ben Jonson's Epicene: *A Retelling*

Ben Jonson's Every Man in His Humor: *A Retelling*

Ben Jonson's Every Man Out of His Humor: *A Retelling*

Ben Jonson's The Fountain of Self-Love, or Cynthia's Revels: *A Retelling*

Ben Jonson's The Magnetic Lady, or Humors Reconciled: *A Retelling*

Ben Jonson's The New Inn, or The Light Heart: *A Retelling*

Ben Jonson's Sejanus' Fall: *A Retelling*

Ben Jonson's The Staple of News: *A Retelling*

Ben Jonson's A Tale of a Tub: *A Retelling*

Ben Jonson's Volpone, or the Fox: *A Retelling*

Christopher Marlowe's Complete Plays: Retellings

Christopher Marlowe's Dido, Queen of Carthage: *A Retelling*

Christopher Marlowe's Doctor Faustus: *Retellings of the 1604 A-Text and of the 1616 B-Text*

Christopher Marlowe's Edward II: *A Retelling*

Christopher Marlowe's The Massacre at Paris: *A Retelling*

Christopher Marlowe's The Rich Jew of Malta: *A Retelling*

Christopher Marlowe's Tamburlaine, Parts 1 and 2: *Retellings*

Dante's Divine Comedy: *A Retelling in Prose*

Dante's Inferno: *A Retelling in Prose*

Dante's Purgatory: *A Retelling in Prose*

Dante's Paradise: *A Retelling in Prose*

The Famous Victories of Henry V: *A Retelling*

From the Iliad *to the* Odyssey: *A Retelling in Prose of Quintus of Smyrna's* Posthomerica

George Chapman, Ben Jonson, and John Marston's Eastward Ho! *A Retelling*

George Peele's The Arraignment of Paris: *A Retelling*

George Peele's The Battle of Alcazar: *A Retelling*

George's Peele's David and Bathsheba, and the Tragedy of Absalom: *A Retelling*

George Peele's Edward I: *A Retelling*

George Peele's The Old Wives' Tale: *A Retelling*

George-a-Greene: *A Retelling*

William Shakespeare's 1 Henry IV, aka Henry IV, Part 1: A Retelling in Prose

William Shakespeare's 2 Henry IV, aka Henry IV, Part 2: A Retelling in Prose

William Shakespeare's 1 Henry VI, aka Henry VI, Part 1: A Retelling in Prose

William Shakespeare's 2 Henry VI, aka Henry VI, Part 2: A Retelling in Prose

William Shakespeare's 3 Henry VI, aka Henry VI, Part 3: A Retelling in Prose

William Shakespeare's All's Well that Ends Well: A Retelling in Prose

William Shakespeare's Antony and Cleopatra: A Retelling in Prose

William Shakespeare's As You Like It: A Retelling in Prose

William Shakespeare's The Comedy of Errors: A Retelling in Prose

William Shakespeare's Coriolanus: A Retelling in Prose

William Shakespeare's Cymbeline: A Retelling in Prose

William Shakespeare's Hamlet: A Retelling in Prose

William Shakespeare's Henry V: A Retelling in Prose

William Shakespeare's Henry VIII: A Retelling in Prose

William Shakespeare's Julius Caesar: A Retelling in Prose

William Shakespeare's King John: A Retelling in Prose

William Shakespeare's King Lear: A Retelling in Prose

William Shakespeare's Love's Labor's Lost: A Retelling in Prose

William Shakespeare's Macbeth: A Retelling in Prose

William Shakespeare's Measure for Measure: A Retelling in Prose

William Shakespeare's The Merchant of Venice: A Retelling in Prose

William Shakespeare's The Merry Wives of Windsor: A Retelling in Prose

William Shakespeare's A Midsummer Night's Dream: A Retelling in Prose

William Shakespeare's Much Ado About Nothing: A Retelling in Prose

William Shakespeare's Othello: A Retelling in Prose

William Shakespeare's Pericles, Prince of Tyre: A Retelling in Prose

William Shakespeare's Richard II: A Retelling in Prose

William Shakespeare's Richard III: A Retelling in Prose

William Shakespeare's Romeo and Juliet: A Retelling in Prose

William Shakespeare's The Taming of the Shrew: A Retelling in Prose

William Shakespeare's The Tempest: A Retelling in Prose

William Shakespeare's Timon of Athens: A Retelling in Prose

William Shakespeare's Titus Andronicus: A Retelling in Prose

William Shakespeare's Troilus and Cressida: A Retelling in Prose

William Shakespeare's Twelfth Night: A Retelling in Prose

William Shakespeare's The Two Gentlemen of Verona: A Retelling in Prose

William Shakespeare's The Two Noble Kinsmen: A Retelling in Prose

William Shakespeare's The Winter's Tale: A Retelling in Prose